P9-ARC-063

THE MYSTERY OF THE

ROGUES' REUNION

"Stop it! Stop it!" Jupiter Jones pleaded. "Turn it off!"

He was staring at a television set. On the screen was a small, plump movie star about three years old called Baby Fatso.

Jupe watched in appalled disbelief. Could that round-faced tot really be him? Jupiter Jones, First Investigator, solver of mysteries that baffled the local police?

It not only could be. Jupe knew it was.

After years of being hidden, Baby Fatso had returned!

The Three Investigators in

THE MYSTERY OF THE
ROGUES' REUNION

by MARC BRANDEL

Based on characters created by
Robert Arthur

RANDOM HOUSE 🏠 NEW YORK

Copyright © 1985 by Random House, Inc.
All rights reserved under International and Pan-American Copyright
Conventions. Published in the United States by Random House, Inc.,
New York, and simultaneously in Canada by Random House of
Canada Limited, Toronto.

Library of Congress Cataloging in Publication Data:

Brandel, Marc
  The Three Investigators in
The mystery of the rogues' reunion.
  (The Three Investigators mystery series ; no. 40)
  "Based on characters created by Robert Arthur."
  SUMMARY: The reunion of a group of child movie stars plunges the
three young detectives into a case of theft, kidnapping, and false identity.
  1. Children's stories, American. [1. Mystery and detective stories] I.
Arthur, Robert. II. Title. III. Title: Mystery of the rogues' re-
union. IV. Series.
PZ7.B7362Thn 1985 [Fic] 84-13395
ISBN: 0-394-86920-6 (pbk); 0-394-96920-0 (lib. bdg.)

Manufactured in the United States of America
    2 3 4 5 6 7 8 9 0

CONTENTS

A FEW WORDS FROM HECTOR SEBASTIAN

Just a moment while I turn off the television set—there.

Now, let me introduce myself. My name is Hector Sebastian. I'm a professional mystery writer, and some of my books have been made into movies.

I don't often watch television, except for the news. But I had a special reason for tuning in to the program I was just watching. A young friend of mine was appearing in it.

I must admit I never would have recognized him. He was much younger when he was an actor in that comedy series, really no more than a baby. But I wanted to watch him because that's how the Mystery of the Rogues' Reunion started.

That mystery is the latest case involving my young friends, the Three Investigators. I'd better tell you a little about them before explaining how they became involved in it.

Their names are Jupiter Jones, Pete Crenshaw, and Bob Andrews. They live in Rocky Beach, a small city on the coast of southern California, not far from my house in Malibu, and only a few miles from Hollywood.

Jupiter Jones—his friends call him Jupe—is the First Investigator. He is a born detective, and I know what I'm talking about because I was a private eye myself before I became a writer. He has those three essential qualities any good detective must have: an eye for noting every detail of a case, an ability to put those clues together and see what they mean, and, most important of all, a dogged determination not to give up until he has come up with the right answer.

I'm not saying Jupe doesn't have some faults. No one has ever accused him of modesty. And he is a little oversensitive in some ways—about his weight, for instance. He doesn't mind if his friends say he's ... well, stocky. But if you want to remain a friend of Jupe's, don't ever, *ever* call him Fatso.

Pete Crenshaw, the Second Investigator, is a natural athlete. He is an excellent runner, swimmer, baseball player. This means that whenever there is anything slightly risky to be done, risky in a physical way, Pete is usually the one who is chosen to do it. Not that he enjoys danger. He doesn't. He is, in fact, the most cautious of the three boys.

Bob Andrews, the Third Investigator, is in charge of records and research. He works part-time at the library in Rocky Beach, and he is naturally studious and thoughtful. He is also very useful to Jupe because he has a way of asking the right questions at the right moment.

Together, the Three Investigators have worked on many cases and solved many bizarre mysteries. But this latest one is a little different from the others. It's different because the First Investigator was personally involved in the Mystery of the Rogues' Reunion.

You see, Jupiter Jones was the child actor I was watching on television just now. He was once one of the Rogues, whose reunion set off the whole mystery.

HECTOR SEBASTIAN

THE MYSTERY OF THE
ROGUES' REUNION

1

JUPE'S
SECRET PAST

"Stop it. Stop it," Jupiter Jones pleaded. "Turn it off."

He was slumped so far down in his swivel chair that only his eyes showed above the battered wooden desk. His voice was a squeak. His usually alert, intelligent face was puckered with pain. The First Investigator looked and sounded like someone who was being tortured. And that's exactly what was happening.

He was being tortured in front of his two best friends. And neither of them was making a move to help him. The other two Investigators, Pete Crenshaw and Bob Andrews, were smiling and chuckling and occasionally laughing out loud.

All three were gathered in their secret Headquarters at The Jones Salvage Yard in Rocky Beach, California, a small coastal city only a few miles from Hollywood. Pete was sprawled in a rocking chair with his feet up on a pulled-out drawer of the filing cabinet. Bob was sitting on a stool, leaning back against the wall.

They were all staring at a television set. On the screen a small, plump child about three years old was sitting cross-legged on a kitchen table. A droopy-eyed boy of eight or nine was holding the child's small, plump hands behind his back. Another boy who might have been eleven was mixing something in a china bowl. He was tall and thin with closely shaved blond hair through which his bony head gleamed like a hard-boiled egg that has been sprinkled with salt. He was grinning in an idiotic way that made you wonder if his hard-boiled egg of a skull had anything inside it except a hard-boiled egg yolk.

"Oh, pleath," the small, plump child said in a surprisingly deep voice. "Pleath, thtop, pleath. I don't wanna have meathles."

"Turn it off," the First Investigator pleaded again. "I can't stand any more of it."

"But I want to see the end," Pete objected. "I want to see how it turnth out. I mean, turns out."

"Come on, Baby Fatso," one of the children on

the screen was saying. He was a sturdily built black boy, about twelve years old, with straight spiky hair that stood out around his head like a porcupine's quills. He was grinning as hard as the others, but there was a gentleness in his smile that made you feel he would never do anything to hurt the fat little boy.

"If your mom and pop think you've got measles," he went on in a singsong voice, "then everyone'll be scared we'll get it too. And we'll all have to stay home from school."

"Yeah," a boy with enormous feet chimed in. "They'll think we're 'fectious."

The boy with the shaved skull, who was known as Bonehead, had finished mixing the liquid in the china bowl and was going into his special comedy routine.

Jupe raised his hand and covered his eyes. He remembered that comedy routine with a particular loathing. Bonehead could wiggle his ears. He could wiggle them so that their huge, pink lobes trembled like blobs of Jell-O.

It was his only talent as an actor, Jupe thought fiercely as Bob and Pete broke into laughter.

Still wiggling his ears, Bonehead picked up a small pointed paintbrush and, dipping it into the bowl, began dabbing red spots on Baby Fatso's plump face. Baby Fatso squirmed and struggled, but he didn't cry. His face remained as cheerful as a spotted cherub's.

Jupe's face didn't. He had opened his fingers so that he could peer between them, and he was watching the screen now with appalled disbelief.

Was that really him? Could that round-faced tot in his cute Farmer Brown overalls, letting Bonehead paint measle spots on his nose and cheeks, really be Jupiter Jones? Jupiter Jones, the First Investigator, solver of mysteries that had sometimes baffled even his friend Chief Reynolds and the local police?

It not only could be. He knew it was. Jupiter had once been Baby Fatso, one of the lead child actors in a series of half-hour comedies featuring the Wee Rogues.

It was a time Jupe tried hard to forget. But when he did occasionally think about it, at odd moments when he had stubbed his toe on a rock or gotten a cinder in his eye, at least he could comfort himself with the thought that Baby Fatso was not a role he had chosen for himself.

When he first became a Wee Rogue at the age of three, Jupiter had been too young to make his own decisions. Not that Jupe blamed his parents for getting him the job. To them it must have seemed like the chance of a show-business lifetime. Until they were killed in an automobile accident when Jupe was four, his parents had been professional ballroom dancers, competing in contests all over California. When they weren't waltzing and tangoing for prize money in glittering ballrooms, they were gracefully dipping and whirling in the background on glittering movie sets. They had appeared together in dozens of musicals at all the big studios.

At one of these studios they had become close friends of the casting director. He occasionally visited them at their home. On one of his visits, a never-to-be-forgotten Sunday afternoon, the casting director had been introduced to their small son, Jupiter.

"You going to be a dancer, too, when you grow up, kid?" the casting director had asked.

"No," Jupe had told him firmly in his precociously deep voice. "My interests are entirely different. I would rather use my mind than my body. I'm afraid my physical coordination isn't very good. On the other hand, my memory is excellent."

"How old did you say he was?" the casting director had asked in the awed voice of a man who has just seen a unicorn in his back garden.

"Two years and eleven months."

The casting director didn't say anything more

about Jupe until just before he left. He seemed to have been struck dumb. "A natural," he had muttered as he was getting into his car. "If ever I saw one, that kid's a natural."

A few days later Jupe was given a screen test. Within a month he had become Baby Fatso and one of the Wee Rogues.

He was an immediate success. Not only was he a natural actor who could hiccup and lisp and laugh and cry in instant obedience to the movie director's orders, he had a talent that none of the other Wee Rogues possessed. He could memorize whole pages of dialogue at a glance. In the year that he acted in the series he never missed a cue or forgot a single line.

If it hadn't been for his parents' tragic death, Jupe might have gone on being a child actor for years. But when his uncle Titus and his aunt Mathilda Jones decided to adopt the orphaned Jupiter and take him to live with them in Rocky Beach, Aunt Mathilda, who was a kind and thoughtful woman, asked Jupiter a kind and thoughtful question.

"Do you want to go on being a Wee Rogue, Jupe?" she inquired.

"Absolutely not," Jupe said.

He didn't mind getting up at half past five every

morning, riding to the studio, or sitting in a chair while the makeup man colored his face and neck and even his ears bright orange to make him look more "natural" on film. He didn't mind endlessly waiting around on the set while the cameraman fussed over the lights. He was perfectly happy reading or doing a crossword puzzle. He didn't even really mind having to make cute remarks or pretending to toddle and lisp. What he couldn't stand was the other Wee Rogues, or most of them.

Unlike Jupiter, they didn't seem to understand that when they were painting measle spots on Baby Fatso's face or watering him with a garden hose to make him tell them where he had hidden his candy, they were supposed to be *acting*. They didn't seem to understand that the mischievous Rogues that people enjoyed on the screen were only made-up characters.

The other Wee Rogues seemed to think that's who they really were. They were always horsing around and telling stupid jokes. Because Jupe was the youngest and the smallest of them, they treated him in the same teasing, bullying way whether the camera was rolling or not.

They put pepper on his ice cream in the studio cafeteria during the lunch break. They spilled glue on his chair in the makeup room. They cut all the buttons off his Farmer Brown overalls.

And worst of all, they called him Baby Fatso. All the time. They couldn't seem to get it through their wooden heads that he wasn't Baby Fatso. Not in real life. He was Jupiter Jones.

So when Aunt Mathilda asked Jupe whether he wanted to go on being a Wee Rogue or not, he didn't hesitate for a second. He felt as though he had been locked in a cage with a bunch of howling, chattering monkeys for longer than he cared to remember, and his kind aunt Mathilda was offering to let him out.

As soon as his first-year contract was up, Jupe quit the Wee Rogues forever. And without him the series soon petered out.

Jupe settled down to living at The Jones Salvage Yard with his uncle and aunt. In grade school he met Pete Crenshaw and Bob Andrews. They became friends and then a little later they became the Three Investigators, serious and professional young private detectives, solving serious and often professional crimes. Jupe did his best to forget he had ever been known as Baby Fatso. And for years he succeeded.

Then a terrible thing happened. Terrible for Jupe anyway. The studio that had made the *Wee Rogues* series sold it as reruns to network television.

The first Jupe knew about it was when a class-mate in school asked him for his autograph. It was shortly after Jupe's name had appeared in the local paper in connection with the rounding up of a gang of pearl thieves in which Jupe had played an important part.

Yours sincerely, First Investigator, Jupiter Jones, Jupe wrote proudly on a blank page of the autograph book.

"No. Your real name," his dim-witted classmate told him, tearing the page out of the book. "The name you're famous for. Baby Fatso."

It had gone on like that for the last three weeks of the school year. Every student at school seemed to have nothing to talk about except the last installment of *The Wee Rogues*. Boys and girls Jupe didn't even know by sight would come up to him in the schoolyard and tell him how funny he was. They would beg him to lisp and chuckle like Baby Fatso. "Say 'Pleath thtop,' pleath," they would plead with him. Jupe's life had become a nightmare.

Things were a little better now that the summer vacation had begun. Jupe could hide from his fans in the Investigators' secret Headquarters in the salvage yard. It was a mobile home that had been buried from view under piles of junk. The trailer now boasted a tiny television set. And that set had become the bane of Jupe's existence. Pete and Bob insisted on watching the reruns of *The Wee Rogues* whenever they could. His pals really *liked* the old series.

Bob and Pete were still smiling and laughing as they watched the television screen now. Bonehead, the skinny kid with the short blond hair, had finished decorating Baby Fatso's face with red spots and was trying to take off his shirt to paint spots on his chest, too. The kitchen door on the screen burst open. A dark-haired little girl of about nine stormed in. This was Pretty Peggy, the heroine of the series and Baby Fatso's faithful champion and rescuer.

"Let him go," Pretty Peggy told Bonehead.

"Yeth, pleath thtop," Baby Fatso chimed in.

Bonehead had no intention of stopping. He tried to lock Pretty Peggy in the closet. Flapjack, the small, sturdy black boy with the porcupine-quill hair, took Peggy's side. In a moment all the Wee Rogues were fighting among themselves. One of them discovered a layer cake on a shelf and threw it at Peggy. It missed her and hit Baby Fatso in the face.

"Oh, yeth," Baby Fatso gurgled, scooping the whipped cream off his nose and stuffing it into his mouth. "That'th much nither than meathles."

"Jupi-ter. Where are you?"

It was Aunt Mathilda's voice over the loud-speaker. Jupe had rigged up a microphone in the yard so he could hear her calling him when he was in Headquarters. Usually when she called him it meant one thing—work. She had a job for him to do. Jupe didn't really mind working around the salvage yard. It helped pay for the boys' private phone in Headquarters. But Jupe didn't exactly enjoy it either. Even now he was more inclined to use his mind than his body.

But today Aunt Mathilda's call was like a reprieve. He jumped up from behind his desk and turned off the television set with a groan of relief. Baby Fatso's gooey face vanished from the screen.

A minute later the Three Investigators had left their carefully concealed Headquarters by the exit known as Secret Four. Walking around a pile of lumber, they approached Aunt Mathilda from behind.

"So there you are," she said.

Jupe started to take off his jacket. "What's the job?" he asked.

But for once Aunt Mathilda had not called the boys to put them to work. There was a man at the gate who wanted to talk to Jupe.

Jupe groaned again, but not with relief. A lot of

people had come to the salvage yard these last few weeks wanting to talk to him. They were newspaper reporters from Los Angeles and even as far away as San Francisco who had tracked him down through the studio and wanted to write feature stories about him. Stories that were going to be headlined WHERE IS HE NOW? or WHATEVER HAPPENED TO BABY FATSO?

"Tell him to go away," Jupe begged Aunt Mathilda. "Tell him I don't want to talk to him."

"I did tell him that, Jupe. But he won't go away. He says it's important." Aunt Mathilda smiled sympathetically. She knew how Jupe felt. She had been busy for weeks now trying to protect him from reporters as well as from dozens of people who wanted him to appear on television talk shows.

"He's got a big comfortable car, Jupe," she went on. "And he says he doesn't care how long he has to sit in it. And he's blocking the driveway. So I guess you'll just have to see him."

"Okay," Jupe agreed reluctantly. "I'll see him and listen to him, just to get rid of him. But I'm not going to talk to him about the Wee Rogues, that's for sure."

It *was* a big comfortable car, a fancy yellow French Citroën with a front end like a whale's head. The man who got out from behind the wheel as the Three Investigators walked through the gate looked big and comfortable too.

As an investigator Jupe had acquired the habit of observing people—their faces, their clothes, the shape of their ears, their little peculiarities. The first thing he observed about this man was his teeth. They were large and white, and they shone like a crescent moon in his suntanned face. They shone whenever he smiled, and he seemed to smile all the time.

"Jupiter Jones," he said with an even bigger smile, "my name's Milton Glass. I'm head of publicity at the studio."

Jupe stood between Pete and Bob, his stocky body rigid with hostility. He scowled at Milton Glass without saying a word.

"I've got an offer I think might interest you, Jupiter." The big man's voice was so friendly that it seemed to be smiling too. "I'm arranging to bring all the Wee Rogues together for an exciting reunion lunch at the studio, and then after the lunch—"

"No, thank you." Jupe couldn't keep silent any longer. This was even worse than he'd expected. The idea of interviews and talk shows was bad enough, but the thought of a reunion with those awful kids made him want to throw up. He turned and started back through the gate into the yard.

"Wouldn't you like to meet all your old friends again?" Milton Glass put his big arm around Jupe's shoulders. "Bonehead and Bloodhound and Footsie and—"

"No, thank you." Jupe tried to break free, but the publicity man had him in a bear-hold. "I saw enough of those idiots to last me the rest of my life and I never—"

"Attaboy." Milton Glass's smile was wider and friendlier than ever. "That's just what I hoped you'd say."

"What?" It wasn't often the First Investigator was thrown off balance, but he couldn't figure out why the big, grinning man seemed so pleased by his refusal. He waited.

"They all picked on you, didn't they? Most of them, anyway. They made you the butt of their stupid practical jokes. They insisted on calling you Baby Fatso all the time. I'll bet you hated them, didn't you?"

"It's not my nature to hate people," Jupe said coldly. "But I certainly disliked them. I disliked them intensely."

"Beautiful." The crescent moon of white teeth shone more brightly than ever in Milton Glass's tanned face. "And now I'm going to give you a chance to get back at them. A chance to show them up as the idiots you always knew they were. Wouldn't you like that?"

"How?" Jupe's face was blank, but there was a gleam of interest in his eyes.

"In front of the whole country. On network television," Milton Glass told him. "The studio's planning a miniseries of two quiz shows. All the Wee Rogues will compete against each other. And my hunch is you'll turn out the winner, Jupiter. You'll make all the rest of them look like dummies."

The First Investigator had a quick flash of remembrance. Bonehead. His hard-boiled egg of a skull. His idiot grin. Bonehead twisting his arm. Bonehead putting a dead mouse in his lunch box.

Jupiter's mind raced as he looked at Milton Glass's friendly, smiling face.

"And the first prize, Jupiter," Milton Glass said encouragingly, "the first prize in the quiz contest is twenty thousand dollars."

2

A SURPRISE AT STAGE NINE

The limousine had to stop at the studio gates on Vine Street in Hollywood. The uniformed guard there nodded familiarly to the chauffeur, then moved to the back of the car to check the three boys' names against a list.

"Jupiter Jones," Jupe told him firmly. He had made up his mind not to stand for any nonsense about being called Baby Fatso.

"Jones, Jupiter." The guard looked at his clipboard. "45 Sunrise Road, Rocky Beach. Right?"

"Right," Jupiter agreed. The guard nodded. Then the other two Investigators had to announce themselves.

"Pete Crenshaw."

"Bob Andrews."

The guard found their names and addresses and nodded again. He stuck a small white card that Jupe recognized as a studio pass under the windshield wiper of the car.

"Stage Nine," he said, waving them on.

The chauffeur of the limousine drove slowly down a long street. Past the New York Public Library. The old San Francisco Opera House. The Leaning Tower of Pisa.

It was all weirdly familiar to Jupe, like a remembered dream. Bob and Pete kept craning forward in their seats to stare at the famous buildings as they passed them. But Jupe knew they weren't really buildings at all. They were only false fronts made of canvas and plaster. If you opened the door of any one of them, there would be nothing behind it.

Jupe sat back in the long black vehicle and didn't even bother to look out the window.

Milton Glass, the publicity man, had sent the limousine to pick Jupe up at the The Jones Salvage Yard. The car and chauffeur would be at Jupe's disposal for the two days of the quiz shows, which they were going to start taping the next day at a television station in Hollywood.

Uncle Titus and Aunt Mathilda had been invited to the preliminary "get together" lunch at the studio. But neither of them had felt like coming.

"Movies are all right," Aunt Mathilda apologized. "I enjoy some of them a lot. But it's like sausages, Jupe. I just don't care to see where they come from or how they're made."

Uncle Titus agreed with her.

Bob and Pete didn't. They jumped at the chance to see what goes on behind the scenes at a movie studio. And Jupe was glad to have them along. It made the First Investigator feel more like himself, his real self, having the other two Investigators with him.

The limousine, which had been crawling along at five miles per hour in obedience to the speed-limit signs, suddenly came to a dead stop. Jupe leaned forward, thinking they had reached the sound stage where the lunch was going to take place. The car had stopped in front of a cluster of wigwams. Two Roman soldiers, carrying spears and shields, were strolling past the tents.

The chauffeur, who had told the boys that his name was Gordon Harker, rolled down his window.

"Could you please tell me how to get to Stage Nine?" he asked one of the soldiers.

Jupe could have told him. Stage Nine was where all the *Wee Rogues* shows had been shot. But for once he didn't feel like displaying his knowledge.

He was in no hurry to get to Stage Nine and his reunion with Bonehead and Footsie and the others.

"It's like just down the street," the Roman soldier
explained, pointing the way with a hand-rolled cig-
arette.

"Yeah, you can't miss it," the other soldier
added.

The chauffeur thanked them and drove on. The
Romans had been right. A huge white building like
an airplane hangar soon loomed up in front of
them. A large figure nine was painted on the side
of it.

The chauffeur jumped out and opened the back
door for the Three Investigators.

Jupe thanked him, looking at the tall, well-built
young man in his smart uniform and cap. As usual,
Jupe's trained investigator's eyes were taking in
everything about Gordon Harker, from his well-
polished shoes to his intelligent, even-featured
black face and straight dark hair.

The entrance to Stage Nine was a small, heavily
padded door. There was a metal clasp at one side of
it with a big, open padlock hanging from a heavy
ring. Without thinking of what he was doing, Jupe
glanced at the two lights above him. Never open the
door when the red light is on, he remembered. It
means they're shooting, the cameras rolling on the

set. It was all coming back to him, all the studio rules and customs from his days as a child actor. He wished it all weren't coming back quite so vividly.

The green light came on. Jupe pushed open the door and stepped inside, followed by Pete and Bob.

It all came back to him even more vividly then. Not only the smell of fresh paint and scorched metal and the dry heat of the arc lamps, but a chorus of raised voices calling those words he had hoped never to hear again.

"Baby Fatso!" the voices shouted.

Jupe found himself surrounded by a group of press photographers. For two or three minutes he stood there patiently while their flashes went off in his face.

And all the time they kept up that awful chant.

"Smile, Baby Fatso."

"Look this way, Baby Fatso."

"One more, Baby Fatso."

At last they were finished. The tall, smiling figure of Milton Glass pushed his way through them and put his bearlike arm around Jupe's shoulders.

"Jupiter," he said cordially. "Jupiter Jones. Come and see the other Wee Rogues."

At the far end of the building was an enormous, brightly lit kitchen. Jupe knew it wasn't really a kitchen, of course. The stove wouldn't work and the faucet in the sink wouldn't yield any water. Only the long table on which several waiters were busy setting up a buffet lunch was not a part of the whole make-believe world of moviemaking.

Milton Glass led Jupe and the other two Investigators to one end of the table where three young men were standing talking to a very attractive young woman with long dark hair.

They all stopped talking and looked at Jupe as he approached them. Jupe looked back at them. He wasn't sure exactly what he had been expecting.

For years he had carried in his mind a clear memory of the other Wee Rogues. But he remembered them as they *had* been. Bonehead, with his hard-boiled egg of a skull and his stupid grin. Footsie with his scrunched-up face like a little sour apple and his overgrown hands and feet. Bloodhound with his long, lolling tongue and his mournful, down-slanted eyes. Pretty Peggy with her black bangs cut straight across her forehead and her small pointed face.

The four adults he was looking at now were complete strangers to him.

One of them—a good-looking young man in a leather jacket with shoulder-length blond hair that covered his ears—raised his hand in a casual greeting.

"Hi," he said. "So they roped you in too, huh?"

Jupe nodded, glancing at the cowboy boots the young man was wearing. They looked unusually small for his six-foot height, so he couldn't be Footsie. He couldn't be Bloodhound either. The young man next to him still had eyes that slanted slightly downward from his nose, although there was no sign of his lolling tongue and he no longer looked in the least mournful.

The sharp-looking character with the leather jacket and the hand-tooled boots had to be Bonehead.

Jupe nodded to the other two Rogues, silently identifying them as Footsie and Bloodhound. They had changed as much as Bonehead had.

Footsie's hands and feet still seemed a little overgrown because he was short and rather thin. But his face had lost the scrunched-up, wrinkled-apple look that had made him stand out as a child actor. His pink cheeks and cheerful eyes reminded Jupe of those friendly guys who worked at the checkout counter at the Rocky Beach supermarket.

Bloodhound reminded Jupe of a young business executive. His brown crew-cut hair, his button-down shirt, and his well-tailored blazer gave him an efficient, on-the-ball appearance. It was difficult to believe he had ever been the sad-faced kid who had played that dopey Bloodhound.

Jupe turned and looked at the young woman in her smart tan suit. She still had a heart-shaped face and deep blue eyes with heavy lashes, but he would never have recognized her on the street as Pretty Peggy.

She smiled at him. "I'm glad you could come, Jupe," she said. "You don't mind if I call you Jupe, do you?"

"Not a bit." Jupe felt pleased that she remembered his real name.

"And you call me Peggy. Never mind the Pretty. I've been trying to live that down for years. Just Peggy, okay?"

"Okay." Jupe looked around for Bob and Pete to introduce them to Peggy and the others. They had walked off the kitchen set and were talking to Milton Glass and a thin, white-haired man who was standing beside a TV camera. The white-haired man looked vaguely familiar to Jupe, but he couldn't immediately place him.

"Now that we're all here"—Bonehead reached out and touched Jupe's arm to draw him closer into the group—"I've got a suggestion to make. Something that's important to every one of us."

"But we're not all here yet," Peggy reminded him. "We're still waiting for Flapjack."

"Flapjack's not coming," Footsie told her.

"Oh, why not?" Peggy sounded disappointed.

Jupe was disappointed too. Of all the Wee Rogues he had liked Flapjack the best. The black kid was the only one, except for Peggy, who hadn't picked on him or tried to make him feel like a fat baby nuisance.

"Either they couldn't find him or he couldn't make it," Bloodhound said with a shrug.

"So we're all here," Bonehead went on. "And we're all here for one thing." He tapped the breast pocket of his leather jacket. "The loot. The money. Right?"

"Right," Bloodhound agreed doubtfully.

"Yeah," Footsie said. "That's the *only* thing we're here for."

Peggy nodded seriously.

"Right?" Bonehead was looking at Jupiter.

Jupe hesitated. Although he would be glad to win the twenty thousand dollars—he could put it aside for his college education—it wasn't strictly true that he had come to the reunion and agreed to compete on the TV quiz show for the sake of the money. He had agreed because he thought it would give him a chance to get back at the kids who had made his life miserable when he was a three-year-old child. But this didn't seem to be the right moment to explain that to them.

"Okay," Jupe said.

"Now, part of the program for this get-together," Bonehead went on, "is that we should all sit around after lunch and have a little rap session about the good old days. Right?"

Peggy nodded again.

They might be the old days, Jupe thought, but he couldn't remember much that was good about them. He didn't say anything.

"And our friendly director over there"—Bone-head flipped his thumb quickly toward the white-haired man who was standing with Milton Glass—"is going to tape us while we talk so they can show it on television before the first quiz show begins."

Jupe glanced quickly over his shoulder. He remembered who the white-haired man was now. His name was Luther Lomax and he had directed every one of the *Wee Rogues* comedies. It wasn't surprising he hadn't recognized the director, Jupe thought. Luther Lomax had changed even more than the Wee Rogues had. Jupe remembered him as a tall, imposing figure who had cracked the whip over all of them with the authority of a lion tamer. "Lights, camera, action!" he used to shout at them. He looked old and stooped and sort of beaten now.

"So, okay." Bonehead was still talking. "If they want us to appear on their television talk show, they'll have to pay us for it. Right?"

He looked at each member of the group in turn again, waiting for an answer.

They all nodded except for Jupe.

"Well?" Bonehead challenged him. "What do you say?"

Jupe paused, thinking hard. If he went along with Bonehead's suggestion, he would be admitting that Bonehead was the leader, the spokesman for them all, as he had once been the ringleader of the awful kids who had played those stupid practical jokes on Jupe as a child.

That idea went against Jupe's whole character. He was used to being the leader himself. As the First Investigator, if he didn't exactly give the other two Investigators orders, at least he made most decisions for them.

On the other hand, he thought Bonehead's suggestion was a pretty good one. If the studio wanted them to appear in a talk-show segment before the first quiz show—even though they would only be talking and not really acting—it made sense that they should be paid for appearing.

Jupe nodded.

Bonehead put his thumb and forefinger in his mouth and gave a piercing whistle.

"Hey, you, Glass," he called across to the publicity man.

Milton Glass walked over to them with his usual brilliant crescent moon of a smile. Luther Lomax, the director, followed him almost timidly. Like an obedient elderly dog walking behind his master, Jupe thought.

"What can I do for you?" Glass inquired politely.

Bonehead told him. He told him clearly and curtly. They each wanted a hundred dollars for the talk-show segment. "And it'll be a fee, not a salary," Bonehead added, "so there'll be no withholding tax. You pay us in cash."

The publicity man's teeth still shone in his tanned face, but a small frown appeared on his forehead.

"I'm afraid that's impossible," he said. "The studio's already gone to a lot of expense for this lunch. And on top of that I've arranged for each of you to receive a valuable souvenir present for being here."

"What kind of present?" Peggy asked him.

"How valuable?" Footsie wanted to know.

"That's a secret, Peggy." Milton Glass turned his smile on her. "But they're all ready and waiting for you out there right now." He gestured toward the kitchen door. "And I know you'll be delighted with them." He paused for a moment. "But there'll be no fees for the talk show," he added firmly.

"Okay." Bonehead didn't even bother to shrug. "No cash. No show."

Milton Glass tried to argue with him. But Bonehead refused to argue back. He explained that it was a take-it-or-leave-it deal. "We're not negotiating, because there's nothing to negotiate."

Glass didn't stop smiling, but his voice was no longer polite.

"That's blackmail," he pointed out. "Sheer, naked blackmail."

"Sure it is." Bonehead smiled back at him, and Jupe saw that Footsie and Bloodhound and even Peggy were smiling too. "That's why you're going to have to pay up."

Milton Glass still didn't agree at once. But Jupe could see that he was going to give in eventually. Jupe was glad enough to get the hundred dollars. It would go into the Three Investigators' fund to pay for the phone at Headquarters and some new equipment he wanted to experiment with. But it wasn't the thought of the money that was occupying his mind.

He was beginning to see the Wee Rogues in a completely different light now, not as he had remembered them for so long. He was beginning to realize that they had all grown up in quite an unexpected way.

They were now a group of tough, competitive young people. People who would use all their wits and experience to fight for what they wanted—money.

And if they would fight like this for a hundred dollars, they would fight as hard and as ruthlessly as a pack of wolves for that quiz-show prize of twenty thousand. Jupe would need every grain of the intelligence and determination he possessed to beat them. Winning the prize money would not be the snap Milton Glass had said it would be.

Jupe realized he no longer hated the other Rogues. It was even hard for him to believe these were the same people who had teased and picked on him years ago. The idea of revenge was fading. But not the idea of winning.

Because it was part of Jupiter's character that he could never refuse a challenge. And it seemed to the First Investigator that he was soon going to be facing one of the biggest challenges of his life.

3

FIVE ROGUES
AND A THIEF

The lunch table had been cleared and carried away. In its place a half circle of swivel chairs had been set up on the movie set of the kitchen.

Milton Glass, who was to be the host of the talk show, sat in the center of the half circle. Peggy was on one side of him and Bonehead on the other. Jupe was sitting at one end next to Bloodhound. Footsie sat at the other end.

The arc lights went on. They glared down on Jupe like a dozen indoor suns. He had eaten very little of the buffet lunch, only a single cold chicken leg and a spoonful of potato salad. Although he normally had a very healthy appetite, he had had to force himself to eat even that much.

It wasn't that he was nervous. He was no more

stage shy now than he had been as a child actor. In the white heat of the lights, facing the peering lenses of the three television cameras, he felt all his natural talent as a performer coming back to him the way a good swimmer feels his abilities when he dives into deep water.

The truth was that the First Investigator's mind had been too busy to be bothered with the thought of food. It was still busy now as the director, Luther Lomax, sitting in the mobile control room, gave the signal to start shooting.

Jupe had a plan that might help him win that quiz-show prize. It was a strategy that seemed to him more likely to work because of the way he had been behaving ever since he had walked into the sound stage. He hadn't done it deliberately. Not at first, anyway. It had just happened. He had hardly said a word to anybody.

All the other Wee Rogues had chatted. But Jupe hadn't joined in. He had only listened. He felt he knew quite a lot about what Bonehead and Footsie and Bloodhound were like now. But they had no way of knowing a thing about him.

"Good evening," Milton Glass said in a cheerful, welcoming voice.

The talk show had started. The three television cameras were rolling, taping as Luther Lomax, watching the monitoring screens in the mobile control room, switched from one camera to another picking the angles he liked best.

"I want you to meet some old friends of yours," Glass went on. "You've all been watching them on this network for several weeks now, and you've been writing us thousands of letters about them, wanting to know what happened to them all, how they turned out in later life. Now you'll be able to find out for yourselves. Because here they are."

He paused for a second and his teeth flashed like sheet lightning.

"The Wee Rogues."

As he spoke a group picture of the kids as they had been was projected on the white wall behind them. Milton Glass went on to explain that he was very sorry, but one of the Wee Rogues, the young man who had played Flapjack, wasn't here today. The studio had done everything it could to find him, but apparently he was no longer living in California and it had been impossible to trace him.

"Maybe he's in jail," Bonehead put in helpfully.

Milton Glass ignored that suggestion except for a slightly embarrassed smile. One by one he asked the Rogues to introduce themselves.

Peggy was first.

"I used to be known as Pretty Peggy," she said. "But that was a long time ago, and as you can all see, I'm just Peggy now."

"Oh, come on." Glass turned his smile on her. "You mustn't be so modest, Peggy. You're still as pretty as a picture."

Peggy didn't smile back at him. "These days I would rather be complimented for my intelligence," she said.

Milton Glass's chuckle sounded a little hollow to Jupe. The First Investigator leaned back in his chair, looking beyond the cameras at the electricians and grips who were gathered around the edge of the set. He could make out Bob and Pete among them. Jupe knew that none of the cameras was focused on him yet, because Bonehead would be the next to introduce himself, so he shrugged slightly and winked at the other two Investigators.

Jupe was signaling them not to be surprised by anything he might do or say when it was his turn to speak. Bob's glasses seemed to flash back an answering signal of support to him.

Jupe's glance moved slightly to the right. He had caught sight of another familiar face in the background. Gordon Harker, the tall, black chauffeur who had driven him to the studio, was walking quietly across the sound stage toward a clump of unused arc lights on their long metal poles.

"I was the one with the shaved skull," Bonehead was saying. "I guess I was supposed to be pretty dumb." He was looking at Milton Glass with his sharp, hard eyes. "Would you say I've changed much?"

You had to hand it to Glass, Jupe thought. The talk-show host didn't lose his good humor for a second. Ignoring Bonehead's obvious hostility, he kept smiling at him as though he were his favorite person in the world.

"You were known as Bonehead, isn't that right?" he asked cheerfully.

"That's right. But then maybe I wasn't as bone-headed as I seemed. Maybe I was just a pretty good actor. Lots of talent."

Bloodhound and Footsie were next. They announced their old movie names as dryly as though repeating their Social Security numbers.

"Bloodhound."

"Footsie."

Milton Glass tried to draw Footsie out a little.

"Why Footsie?" he asked. "Why were you known as Footsie?"

"Because that's what they called me."

"Yes, but why?"

"That's what it said in the script."

Milton Glass's smile dimmed by fifty watts for just a moment.

It was Jupe's turn next.

"And who were you?" Milton Glass demanded jovially.

Jupe smiled back at him.

"I'm J-J-Jupiter Jones," he stammered.

"Yes, that's who you are now. But who were you then?"

"J-J-Jupiter Jones. I've always been Jupiter J-J-Jones."

Jupe's forehead was creased with a puzzled frown. As an investigator he had often found it useful to pretend to be stupid. It was a role he was good at. But he had never played it as skillfully as he did now. He put all his acting talent into appearing too dumb to understand some of the questions that were put to him. When Milton Glass asked him what part he had played in the *Wee Rogues* comedies, Jupiter looked blank and shook his head.

"I was just a b-b-baby," he stammered at last. "I don't remember m-m-much about it."

The talk-show host finally had to make the introduction himself.

"Jupiter Jones was Baby Fatso," he announced.

"And many people think he was the finest actor among the Wee Rogues."

With the introductions over, Milton Glass began to ask his guests what they were doing now.

"I'm a receptionist," Peggy told him, "in San Francisco."

"I'm sure you're a very good one. It must give people a big lift to walk into an office and see your pretty face. You must get a lot of friendly smiles."

"Not me." Peggy shook her head. "Did you ever see anyone smile in a *dentist's* office?"

Glass seemed to have come to a dead end. He tried another tack.

"So you didn't pursue your career in show business." He beamed. "You gave all that up?"

"It gave me up," Peggy contradicted him quietly. "I haven't been offered a job in movies since I was ten years old."

"I expect your parents wanted you to go to school and live an ordinary life. . . ."

Peggy shook her head again. "No, they didn't. They were always trying to push me back into acting. Anyway, by then it was impossible for me to live an ordinary life."

Glass didn't ask her why. Peggy told him anyway.

"For years people kept recognizing me on the

street. 'Aren't you Pretty Peggy? I remember you. Oh, you were so cute.' Until I was afraid to go out of the house. And it was even worse in school. Would you like me to tell you the truth?"

Her host nodded, still smiling, although there was a look in his eyes that made Jupe think that the truth was the last thing Milton Glass wanted to be told.

"If I ever have a child, I'd sooner see it become a gravedigger than an actor. It's steadier work and there's more future in it."

"Speaking of the future," the talk-show host said, grabbing at the chance to change the subject, "have you any special plans for *your* future, Peggy?"

For once Peggy smiled back at him. There was a wistful eagerness in her smile.

"Yes," she said. "I'd like to go to college if I can ever get enough money together. I'm sick of being just a pretty face. I'd like to develop my mind so I can do something interesting and useful with my life."

"I'm sure you will."

With a beam of relief, Glass swiveled in his chair so that he was facing Bonehead.

If he had expected to have an easier, jollier time with Bonehead than he had with Peggy, he was soon disappointed. It turned out that Bonehead was now working as a mechanic in a garage. He insisted on describing his job in some detail.

"I lie flat on my back under other people's cars and the oil drips in my eyes and the grease gets under my fingernails and my arms get so tired reaching up with those wrenches. . . ."

"How would you feel about getting back into movies?" Glass was trying to steer him onto a more cheerful subject. "After all, you said yourself you were a pretty good actor as a kid."

"*Acting.*" Bonehead seemed to spit the word at him. "You know how many actors are out of work in this town?"

Apparently Milton Glass didn't. Or if he did, he didn't want to talk about it.

"Did you ever have the same kind of trouble as Peggy?" he asked instead. "Being recognized on the street?"

Bonehead had to admit that he hadn't. "After the studio stopped shaving my head, and I let my hair grow long like this to hide my famous wiggling ears, I guess I looked so different my own mother wouldn't have recognized me."

Milton Glass didn't ask Bonehead if he had any special plans for the future. As far as Jupe was concerned, he didn't need to. Jupe felt he already knew what Bonehead's immediate plans were. To win that twenty-thousand-dollar prize money by any means he could.

The talk-show host went on to Footsie and Bloodhound. Footsie was unemployed "most of the time." But Bloodhound turned out to be a pleasant surprise for Milton Glass. He had graduated from high school and was in his first year of college.

"I guess I was lucky," he said. "My father's a lawyer. And he never really wanted me to be a child actor, anyway. A client of his, who was a producer at the studio, convinced him to do it. Once my father saw what a grind it was, he was sorry he'd roped me into it."

Glass asked Bloodhound if having a famous face had made it tough for him in school.

"It did for a while," Bloodhound remembered. "I used to have those droopy eyes. But when I got to be about fourteen, they stopped drooping so much. And by then people had forgotten about the Wee Rogues anyway."

It was Jupe's turn again.

"And what are *you* doing now?" Milton Glass inquired.

Jupe stared at him blankly. "I'm not doing anything. I'm just sitting here," he said.

"I mean what are you doing with your life?"

"Oh," Jupe said. "Oh, I live in Rocky B-B-Beach."

"But what do you do there?"

That question seemed to puzzle Jupe. He scratched his head and wriggled in his chair. Then he admitted at last that he sometimes went swimming at the b-b-beach.

"But don't you go to school?" It seemed nothing could dull the brilliance of Milton Glass's smile, but there was an unmistakable note of impatience in his voice.

"N-n-not during summer vacation," Jupe informed him.

Glass gave up on him after that. He did not ask what plans Jupe had for his future.

The first part of the talk show was over, but there were still six minutes to fill.

Glass turned his smile on the cameras.

"Now, I'm going to ask our guests to talk about the past," he announced. "I'm sure they all have some amusing and interesting stories to tell about the old days when they were the Wee Rogues."

Once again Peggy led off.

"Most of all, I remember the hairdresser," she said. "She used to brush my hair so hard it made my head ache."

Bonehead remembered his paycheck.

"We used to get it on Friday nights," he recalled. "They paid us in cash in those days. In a brown envelope fastened with a piece of red string."

"I expect that was a particularly happy time for you, wasn't it?" Milton Glass prompted him.

"Not for me," Bonehead contradicted him. "For my old man. It was the only time he ever came to the studio. So he could grab the loot away from me."

Footsie remembered having to wear big floppy shoes. "They had to stuff them with tissues so they wouldn't fall off," he went on. "And they were still so loose they gave me blisters."

Bloodhound remembered the days he didn't have to work at the studio. "My father used to take the afternoon off too," he said, "and we'd go to a ball game or down to the beach. Boy, we were both counting the weeks until my contract ran out."

Jupe didn't seem to be able to remember anything at all. "I was just a b-b-baby," he explained again. He said he had no memory of ever having acted. He had never heard of Baby Fatso until he had seen him on television a few weeks before. "And then someone told me that was m-m-me," he said.

"That must have been quite a revelation to you,"

Glass prompted him with his hollow chuckle.

He had chosen an unfortunate word. Jupe obviously didn't understand what a revelation was. By the time his host had explained the word to him, there were only three minutes left.

Glass stood up, facing the cameras.

"And now I've got a surprise for you all," he said, beaming. "To thank the Rogues for appearing on this talk show, I'm going to present each and every one of them with a token of the studio's appreciation. Trixie, if you please."

He turned his head slightly as a very pretty young blonde in a short skirt entered through the door of the kitchen. She was carrying a large square box wrapped in golden paper.

She held the box out to Milton Glass while he untied the ribbon and removed the wrapping.

He paused for a second before lifting off the lid.

"You're each going to receive a very valuable gift," he announced with his widest, warmest smile, "which I hope you will treasure for the rest of your lives."

He paused again before telling them what the gift was.

"A sterling-silver loving cup engraved with your name and the title of the series that you have helped make such a tremendous success—*The Wee Rogues.*"

He removed the lid and handed it to Trixie. He peered into the box. He plunged his hand into it. He grabbed the box and shook it. It fell out of his hands and bounced across the floor before it settled with its open end facing the cameras.

The box was empty. There were certainly no valuable silver loving cups in it.

The First Investigator was watching the talk-show host's face. For the first time since Jupe had met him, Milton Glass was not smiling.

4

THE LIGHT
STRIKES

"It's not on," Bob said.

"Are you sure you've got the right channel?" Pete asked.

Bob nodded. "They were supposed to show it at a quarter to five, just before the news. It was announced in the paper. But there's nothing but an old Western."

After being driven back to Rocky Beach in the chauffeured limousine, the Three Investigators had gone straight to Headquarters.

Pete sat down in the rocking chair and put his feet up. "I guess they decided to cancel it after those cups got stolen," he suggested. "What do you think, Jupe?"

Jupiter didn't answer. He was slumped down in

46

his chair behind the desk, pinching his lower lip. It was an old habit. He said it helped him think, and he was thinking hard now.

Bob turned off the television set on which he had been trying to get the scheduled broadcast of "The Wee Rogues Talk Show." Two galloping cowboys wearing black hats vanished from the screen.

"They're still there," Jupe said thoughtfully.

"Who?" Bob sat on his stool and leaned back against the wall.

"Not who—what," the First Investigator corrected him. "Those five silver loving cups they were going to give us. They're still there."

"Still where?" Pete asked.

"They searched everybody before we left Stage Nine," Jupe explained. "And they searched the limousine again at the studio gate. Whoever stole the cups could never have managed to get them out. So they're still there, hidden somewhere in that sound stage."

"What's it called a sound stage for anyway?" Pete wanted to know.

"Because," Jupe explained, "years ago when movies started to talk, all the studios had to sound-proof their sets."

"Well, I guess you're right about the cups," Pete said. He knew from experience that the First Investigator was almost always right when he came up with one of his pieces of deduction. "But what do you care? You didn't really want yours, did you? What would you do with a silver loving cup anyway?"

"Especially the way you feel about the Wee Rogues," Bob reminded him. He smiled, remembering Jupe's performance that afternoon. "You certainly showed that Milton Glass what you thought of his whole publicity stunt, the way you played dumb on that show."

"I wasn't trying to show Milton Glass anything." Jupe answered thoughtfully. "I was simply trying to reassure Bonehead and Bloodhound."

"How?" Pete couldn't quite figure out what his friend was talking about.

"It's like fencing," Jupe told him. "If you think the man you're up against doesn't know a sword from a scabbard, you may be tempted to let your guard down."

"Say it in English," Pete suggested. Jupiter did tend to talk in a way that was too complicated for the other two Investigators to follow.

"If the other contestants on the quiz show think I'm too stupid to remember my own name," Jupe explained patiently, "they're not going to be trying so hard to beat me."

"Yeah," Pete agreed. "I see what you mean."

Bob was polishing his glasses. He nodded admiringly. It did all seem to make sense now.

"However," Jupe continued after a moment, "the theft of those loving cups seems to have changed things a little."

"You mean we've got a case to investigate now," Bob said. "Is that what you mean, Jupe?"

He knew that once Jupe was presented with a puzzle, any puzzle, nothing could distract him until he had solved it. Bob felt a little the same way himself, and Pete did too. After all, they did call themselves The Three Investigators, and no genuine investigator would ever turn his back on a case. If something had been stolen, it was an investigator's job to find out who had taken it.

"Got any ideas, Jupe?" Pete inquired.

The First Investigator didn't answer. He was reaching for the phone. Referring to a business card, he dialed a number.

"Hello," he said. "Easy-Ride Limos? Jupiter Jones here. One of your drivers has been assigned to me for the Wee Rogues quiz shows. His name is Gordon Harker. Could I speak to him, please?"

There was silence before the chauffeur was put on the line.

"Hello, Mr. Harker," Jupe said. "I'm sorry to

bother you again. But I just got a call from the studio and they want me to go back there. . . . Yes, right away. . . . Okay, thank you. We'll be waiting at the gate."

"We're going out to the studio again?" Pete took his feet down and stood up. "But how are we going to get in, Jupe? I mean, they're not expecting us. They didn't really call you, did they?"

"No, I'm afraid that was stretching the truth a little." Jupe reached in his pocket and pulled out a slip of paper. "But they'll let us in because I've got the studio pass. I took it off the windshield of the limousine when it dropped us back here. I was afraid the chauffeur, Gordon Harker, might want to use it."

He didn't explain himself any further than that for the moment. And when Bob and Pete tried to question him during the drive to the studio, he shook his head quickly, signaling them to keep quiet.

At the studio gates Jupe showed his pass to the guard, who waved them on at once without any questions. The limousine moved down the street of famous buildings, deserted now, and stopped in front of the door of Stage Nine. Gordon opened the rear door for the boys.

"We'll probably only be a few minutes, half an hour at most," Jupe told the chauffeur.

"Okay." Gordon Harker slid back into the driver's seat. "I'll be just down the street here when you need me."

Jupe waited until the car had pulled away before walking to the small padded door. He knew it wouldn't be padlocked. The sound stages were always kept open, he remembered from his days as a child actor, so that the night shift of studio workers, which came on at 8 P.M., could take down a set or put up a new one for the next day's shooting.

Inside, the huge sound stage was in almost complete darkness. Only a few dim bulbs in wire cages dangled from the gantry, the high metal balcony that ran around the top of the vast building.

Jupe slipped a flashlight from his pocket and shone it ahead of him as he made his way over the tangle of electrical cables that littered the floor.

Bob and Pete followed him to the kitchen set at the far end. The First Investigator paused there, shining his flashlight around the walls.

"Now, let's see," Jupiter Jones said so softly that he might have been talking to himself. "The buffet table was here. And then right after lunch they carried it out that way and set up the swivel chairs for the talk show. And all that time the golden box with the loving cups in it must have been just outside the set. . . ."

He walked to the door in the set. It was through that door that the young blond woman had entered when it was time for Milton Glass to make the presentation.

Jupe opened the door and walked through it, followed by his friends.

"It was probably sitting there. . . ." Jupe's flashlight picked out a sturdy table a few feet away from him. "But that door was never opened while we were in the kitchen until the box was brought in. The waiters and the cameramen and everybody else came into the kitchen the way we did, through the open end of the set. And there were grips and electricians and a whole crowd of people standing around there all the time. So . . ." He looked at Bob and Pete. "What do you think?"

"So whoever stole the cups couldn't have smuggled them into the kitchen and hidden them there," Pete suggested. "He would have had to take the cups out of the box and walk through the crowd at the open end of the set into the kitchen."

"Right." Jupe nodded. "So let's assume I'm the thief." He walked around the end of the canvas flats that formed the walls of the kitchen to the open space where the camera crew had gathered during the buffet lunch.

"I'm here, and I'm surrounded by people," he went on. "But if I slip over to that table with the box on it, I'm out of sight behind the set." Shining his flashlight in front of him, he walked back to the table.

"The door into the kitchen is closed, and there's no reason for anyone else to come back here," he said thoughtfully. "So with any luck I've got plenty of time to open the box, take out the cups, and re-seal the gold wrapping paper."

He went through the motions of doing it with his hands.

"So I'm standing here with five silver cups," he continued. "I may have a sack or something to put them in. But there are all those people just around the end of the set, so . . ."

"So you have to hide them somewhere around here," Bob finished for him. He switched on his own flashlight and let the beam play over the area, picking out a coil of cables, several large cans of paint, a stack of two-by-fours, and, slightly to one side, a heavy wooden chest.

Jupe stood where he was, keeping his flashlight on them, while the other two Investigators made straight for the wooden chest.

There was nothing in it except some carpenter's tools. There was nothing under the two-by-fours either or in any of the empty paint cans.

Bob and Pete turned and looked at the First Investigator. He wasn't watching them. He was standing beside one of the movable arc lights and examining the hand screw on its tall metal pole.

Jupe stiffened suddenly, looking up several feet above him at the big black box that housed the reflector.

"Give me a hand with this," he said.

The other two Investigators hurried over to him. They loosened the screw that held the pole in its extended position, then lowered the reflector box slowly until Jupe could reach it. He found the catch and pulled open the side of the box. He reached inside.

Suddenly a hundred bolts of lightning seemed to strike all at once, merging into one lasting flash.

The whole end of the sound stage where the kitchen set stood was flooded with light!

5

A SUSPECT
SURFACES

The Three Investigators stood motionless in the
glare of the arc lights. Bob and Pete were still grip-
ping the metal pole. Jupe had his hand inside the
reflector box.

"Okay," a commanding voice said. "Just stay
where you are."

The boys stayed still as Luther Lomax, the director of *The Wee Rogues*, moved away from the master control switch box and walked across the sound
stage toward them.

He halted a few feet away, his eyes fixed on Jupe.
There was no need for any flashlight now. They
could all see the inside of the reflector case. They
could see Jupe's hand reaching into it. They could

see the five silver cups in the space behind the reflector.

"So that's where you hid them," Luther Lomax said. He had seemed old and beaten that afternoon at the lunch, but there was a tone of authority in his voice now that reminded Jupe of the way he had ordered the Wee Rogues around when he had been directing the series.

"Those cups cost the studio two thousand dollars," Lomax went on. "And the three of you sneaked them out of their box this afternoon and hid them in that arc light when no one was looking."

"No," Jupiter Jones said. "I didn't hide them here, Mr. Lomax. I just found them here." He took the silver cups out of the space behind the reflector and handed them, one by one, to the director.

"You'll have to think up a better story than that." Lomax put the cups on the table. "The only one who would know where to find those things would be the person who stole them."

"I didn't steal them." The First Investigator raised his voice a little. He was feeling thoroughly indignant. "I simply managed to figure out where the thief put them. Bob and Pete and I were sitting around at Headquarters discussing the case and—"

"Headquarters?" the director interrupted him

sharply. "What do you mean, 'Headquarters'?"

"It's our office at home," Jupe explained. "It's where we meet to work on our cases."

"What cases?" Luther Lomax had raised his voice too. "You'll be telling me you're police detectives next."

"No, we're not police detectives," Jupe admitted. "But we are investigators."

He took a business card from his shirt pocket and gave it to the director. He had printed it himself on an old handpress Uncle Titus had bought as junk for his salvage yard. On the card it said:

THE THREE INVESTIGATORS
"We Investigate Anything"
? ? ?

First Investigator .... Jupiter Jones
Second Investigator .... Peter Crenshaw
Records and Research .... Bob Andrews

Under that was the private phone number of their Headquarters in the junkyard.

People often asked what the three question marks stood for. The answer was—mysteries unsolved, riddles unanswered. Luther Lomax didn't ask anything. He looked at the card as though it were a wooden nickel.

"That doesn't prove a thing," he said. "You could have a card printed saying you were the president of the studio. It certainly doesn't prove you didn't steal these cups."

"But we didn't," Bob insisted. "When we came here, we didn't even know where they were hidden."

"We thought they might be in one of those paint cans," Pete said, backing him up.

"And then Jupe figured out they were in that arc light," Bob went on. "How, Jupe? I mean how did you figure it out?"

"It was too high," the First Investigator explained absently. "It was the only light whose pole was extended to its full length. And I wondered why."

He spoke as though his mind was on something else. He was looking at the director in a thoughtful way. The truth was he was trying to think of some way of convincing Luther Lomax that he and Bob and Pete actually were investigators and not thieves. It was obvious the director wasn't going to believe *them*. But there might be someone else he would listen to.

"Mr. Lomax, do you know Hector Sebastian?" Jupe asked.

"The mystery writer? I've heard of him. Why?"

"He's a good friend of ours. And he knows all about us, about our being investigators. He's taken a lot of interest in our cases."

The director was still holding the Three Investigators card in his hand. He scrunched it impatiently and dropped it on the floor.

"What do you expect me to do?" he demanded. "Ask Hector Sebastian to give you a reference?"

"Why not?"

Lomax hesitated. "I've never even met the man and I don't know his phone number."

"I do." Jupe took a pencil and another of his business cards from his pocket and wrote the number on the back of it. "I'm sure he wouldn't mind your calling him," he said.

Lomax still hesitated for a second, then walked over to the phone on the far wall of the sound stage.

The Three Investigators watched him while he dialed the number and then, although they couldn't hear what he was saying at that distance, they could see him talking on the phone. He talked for a surprisingly long time.

He was smiling when he finally hung up and walked back to them.

"He remembered my name," the director said in a surprised but pleased voice. "I didn't think he would. You see, when the studio was going to make a film of his novel, *Dark Legacy,* I was hoping to direct it, and then . . ." He shrugged in a resentful way. "And then the studio decided to put a younger man on it." He smiled again. "It was a few years ago, but he remembered at once who I was. Hector Sebastian remembered my name."

"But what did he say about us?" Pete asked.

"Oh." Luther Lomax shook his head as though to bring himself back to the present. "Oh, yes. It's okay. He said you couldn't possibly have stolen those cups. So if you want to go home now, I'll see they're returned to the publicity department."

Jupe thanked him for making the call.

"Not at all," the director assured him. "It was a great pleasure talking to Hector Sebastian. People forget you so fast in this business. But he remembered everything about me, all the fine movies I've directed."

Jupe signaled to Pete and Bob and they all walked across the sound stage to the exit door, leaving the director still lost in his own thoughts as he stood in the light of the kitchen set.

"What do you think, Jupe?" Pete asked as they stepped out into the street.

The First Investigator didn't answer at once. He was pinching his lower lip.

"Who do you think did it?" Bob prompted him.

"Who do you think stole those silver cups?"

"Those arc lights," Jupe said thoughtfully. "Someone had to be sure they wouldn't be used." He stopped and the other two Investigators halted beside him in the shadow of the huge sound stage. "Maybe that's why he waited until the cameras were rolling. . . ." He frowned. "But I'm not sure."

"Bonehead?" Pete suggested. "Or maybe Footsie?"

"I'm not sure," Jupiter Jones repeated. "There are several rather puzzling aspects to this whole case."

"Yes? What?" Bob wanted to know.

"For one thing . . ." The First Investigator tapped his thumb with the finger of his other hand. "Puzzle number one: our chauffeur, Gordon Harker."

"Why?" Pete asked. "What's puzzling about him?"

"His memory," Jupe explained. "The guard at the gate this morning recognized him, so Harker obviously does quite a lot of driving for the studio. But he didn't remember where Stage Nine was. He had to ask someone."

The First Investigator started forward again toward the parked limousine at the end of the street.

"Unless Harker was only pretending," he said. "Unless he knew all about those silver cups that were going to be presented to us on the talk show. And he wanted *us* to think he didn't even know where that sound stage was."

"You mean you think he stole them?" Bob asked.

Jupe frowned. "I'm not accusing anyone," he answered thoughtfully, "not yet, anyway. But I did see Gordon Harker walk around the back of that kitchen set . . . just before the talk show began."

6

JUPE DOES SOME SLEUTHING

As soon as he had finished his breakfast the next morning and helped Aunt Mathilda wash the dishes, Jupiter Jones walked out to his workbench in the salvage yard. He was due at the television station at two o'clock that afternoon to tape the first of the two quiz shows.

In most quiz shows, he knew, the contestants are allowed to choose their own subjects. There would be several categories: history, sports, famous people, and so on. Each Wee Rogue would be allowed to choose one of them and then answer questions about that one area.

As he paused by his workbench Jupe was wondering what the categories would be on "The Wee Rogues Quiz Show." He hoped one of them would be science, his best subject in school.

Peggy had tried to question Milton Glass about that at the buffet lunch yesterday, but the publicity man had clammed up at once and refused to tell them anything about how the quiz would be run or what sort of questions to expect.

"It's a surprise," he had said.

Scattered on the workbench, which was sheltered by a tin roof, were the parts of several old broken cameras that Uncle Titus had brought home one day. Using the lens of one and the shutter of another, Jupe was fitting them together to make what he intended to be a special "investigator's" secret camera—one that could be hidden under the lapel of his jacket and take pictures through his buttonhole. He was very clever with his hands and he enjoyed making new things out of old bits and pieces.

He had only been working for a few minutes when he straightened suddenly and put down his tools. A red light was blinking over the workbench. That meant the phone was ringing in Headquarters.

A few feet from him an old metal grating just seemed to be leaning against a pile of junk. Jupe quickly lifted the grating aside. Beyond it was the entrance to a large corrugated pipe. This was Tunnel Two, one of the secret entrances to Headquarters.

As fast as he could, Jupe squeezed his stocky body through the pipe and pushed his way up through a trap door into the trailer.

He scooped up the phone. "Jupiter Jones speaking."

"This is Luther Lomax. I hope you don't mind my calling you."

It was strange, Jupe thought, how Luther Lomax's voice changed from one moment to the next. Last night on the sound stage when he had accused Jupe and his friends of stealing those silver cups, Lomax's voice had had all the authority and command that Jupe remembered from his days as Baby Fatso. Then a few minutes later when Lomax was talking about being replaced as the director on Hector Sebastian's movie, *Dark Legacy,* Lomax had sounded tired and defeated. He sounded a little that way now.

"Not at all," Jupe said. "I'm glad to hear from you, Mr. Lomax. I was wondering if you had found out who did steal those silver cups."

"No. Not yet. At least, not exactly. That's what I wanted to talk to you about." A little of the authority was coming back into the director's voice. "It's too complicated to go into over the phone, and I was wondering if you could come to the television station early so we could sit down and discuss it."

"Sure," Jupe said. "What time would you like me to be there?"

"Come at eleven. Eleven sharp. Just ask for me at the reception desk." He paused briefly. "Are your two friends with you?"

"No, I'm afraid I'll have to come alone," Jupe told him.

It was too bad, he thought as he hung up, that he couldn't get the other two Investigators to come with him this early. He knew they were spending the morning on the beach. They had asked him to go too, but he hadn't felt like a long bike ride and a strenuous swim in the surf. He had wanted to be as rested as possible for the quiz show.

He called Bob's mother and told her of his change of plan, promising to send the limo back to pick up Bob and Pete so that they could get to the television station in time for the taping.

When Jupe called the limousine company, Gordon Harker answered the phone himself. He agreed to meet Jupe at the salvage yard in thirty minutes.

Jupe changed into a dark suit with a white shirt and a tie and was waiting at the gate when the chauffeur drew up. They drove into Hollywood in silence. But when they reached the big television network office building and the chauffeur opened the car door for him, Jupe could see from the hesitation in Gordon Harker's face that there was something on his mind. Something he wanted to ask Jupe.

The First Investigator waited, standing on the sidewalk.

"I've never seen a quiz show," Harker began. "They have live audiences, don't they?"

"Yes," Jupe said. "I guess there'll be a couple of hundred people watching this one."

"It should be interesting." The chauffeur shifted his feet in an embarrassed way. "Do you happen to have a spare ticket?" he asked.

Jupe did. Milton Glass had given him four tickets in case he wanted to invite his family to the show. Aunt Mathilda and Uncle Titus had politely declined. Bob and Pete had two of the tickets. And Jupe still had the others in his pocket. He offered one of them to Gordon Harker.

"Thanks." The chauffeur took it eagerly. "Thanks a lot. I'll pick up your two friends later and then come and watch the quiz. And . . . well, good luck."

As Jupe entered the office building, he was frowning thoughtfully. Gordon Harker was more and more of a puzzle to him. Why should an intelligent man like Harker want to come watch a bunch of ex-child actors answer a lot of stupid questions And why had he seemed so shy about it? Maybe the man was spellbound by the supposed glamor of show business, Jupe decided. That happened to a lot of otherwise sensible people.

The receptionist sent Jupe straight up to Luther Lomax's office. GUEST DIRECTORS, it said on the door. The elderly director seemed glad to see him. Jupe sat down facing him across the desk.

"When I was talking to Hector Sebastian last night," Lomax began, "he gave you an excellent reference. I don't mean just a character reference. He told me at once, of course, that you couldn't possibly have stolen anything." He paused for a moment. "Do you mind if I call you Jupiter?"

"Most people call me Jupe," the First Investigator told him.

"Jupe, then," the director went on. "Hector Sebastian also said that you have a real talent as a detective. He mentioned that you and your friends have solved several baffling mysteries."

Jupe nodded. Modesty was not one of his outstanding qualities, and it was pleasant to hear that his friend Hector Sebastian shared his own high opinion of his abilities.

"So it occurred to me, Jupe . . ." Lomax paused briefly. "Since the movie studio naturally doesn't want any publicity about the theft of those cups, since the studio doesn't even want to report the matter to the police . . ." He paused again. "It occurred to me that this might be a perfect case for you and your two friends to handle. If you can find out who the thief was, there might even be a small reward for you."

Jupiter thanked him. "We'd be most interested in taking the case, even without a reward," he added.

"Good." Lomax ran his fingers through his thin white hair. "Then between ourselves—and this is in the strictest confidence, Jupe—I may as well tell you that I have a strong suspicion about who did steal those cups."

Jupe didn't say anything. He waited for the director to go on.

"When I was leaving the sound stage last night," Lomax told him, "I saw someone running away from the door. Someone who must have been startled by my footsteps. It was pretty dark when I got outside, but I saw a young man hurrying toward the studio gates."

Jupe waited again.

"I couldn't see his face," the director explained, "but his walk was immediately familiar to me. The way he turned his feet out, like Charlie Chaplin. It was that boy who used to play the part of Footsie."

"Do you think he came to the sound stage to retrieve the cups?" Jupe asked.

The director nodded. "It's the obvious answer, isn't it? What other reason could he possibly have for being there?"

Jupe couldn't think of any. "But that doesn't exactly prove that Footsie was the thief, does it?" he asked.

"No, but it's a very strong lead." The authority was back in the director's voice. He straightened his shoulders. "Perhaps I had no right to do this. But today being Saturday with no shooting at the studio, I knew that the sound stage wouldn't be used again until Monday. So when I left, I padlocked the door."

He took a key from his pocket and put it on the desk.

"My hunch is that Footsie did steal those cups," he said firmly. "And I think he'll go back to that sound stage, hoping to find it unlocked. Hoping to find those cups still hidden in that arc light."

"You may be right," Jupe said. "After all, he has no way of knowing that we've already found them."

"No. The publicity department has strict orders to say nothing about it." The director pushed the key across the desk toward Jupe. "Take it," he said. "And keep your eye on Footsie. Maybe you can find some way of trapping him. And now, if you'll excuse me, I've got some things to do before the show."

Jupe took the key and stood up.

"Keep your eye on Footsie," Luther Lomax repeated as the First Investigator left the office.

Outside in the corridor Jupe glanced at his watch. He still had almost two hours to kill before he was due in the television studio upstairs. He took the elevator back to the lobby and made himself comfortable on a sofa in the corner. People kept moving in and out through the street doors, pausing at the reception desk, heading for the elevators.

Suddenly Jupe leaned forward, shielding his face with his hands.

There he was, the very person Jupe had been told to keep an eye on.

He saw Footsie walk past him and step into an elevator. He saw the door close behind him. Jupe stood up and watched the indicator panel as the lights flashed on and off, pausing occasionally as the elevator stopped at various floors.

It stopped several times. There was no way Jupe could tell at which floor Footsie had gotten out. There was no sense in trying to go after him. Jupe walked back to the sofa and sat down again.

One thing the First Investigator did know: The

television studio where the quiz show was going to be taped was on the seventeenth floor and the elevator hadn't stopped there. Footsie hadn't been on his way to the studio, so there was a chance he was simply visiting someone in the building. There was a chance he might come back through the lobby.

Jupe decided to stay where he was, to wait and see. He didn't have long to wait. In less than five minutes Footsie walked past him again, carrying an envelope. He headed out to the street.

Keeping well behind so as not to be seen, Jupiter followed him. As he stepped out onto the sidewalk he was just in time to see Footsie pull an old motorbike away from the curb, jump onto it, and splutter away down the boulevard in the direction of the movie studio on Vine Street.

Jupe looked around. A few yards away an elderly woman was getting out of a taxi in front of the network building. Jupe waited until she had paid the fare, then he jumped into the back of the cab.

"Where to?" the driver asked him.

Jupe leaned forward, thinking fast. If Footsie was going to the sound stage, as Jupe thought he was, there was no point in following him there. It would be much better for Jupe to get there first and hide himself on the sound stage before Footsie arrived.

He gave the driver the address of the movie stu-

dio on Vine Street. From the sound of that motorbike's sputtering engine he was sure the taxi could
get there much faster than Footsie could.

He was right. The cab passed the motorbike at
the second stoplight. The studio was only two miles
farther on, just off Hollywood Boulevard.

Jupe paid the cab driver at the studio gates,
showed his pass to the guard, and hurried down the
deserted street of famous buildings to the door of
Stage Nine. Using the key Luther Lomax had given
him, he unfastened the padlock and stepped inside.

It was completely dark in the vast sound stage.
Jupe wished he had brought his flashlight with him.
But there was no time to waste on regret. If Footsie
was on his way to retrieve the stolen silver cups, he
would be there any second now.

Leaving the heavily padded door open a few
inches to give himself some light, Jupe started to
grope his way toward the kitchen set at the far end
of the huge building. He had gone less than ten
yards when he heard a soft thud behind him. He
turned quickly, looking back toward the door.

There was no gleam of light showing from it now.
It had been shut from the outside.

As quickly as he could in the total darkness, the
First Investigator found his way back to the padded
door. He pushed against it. He pushed harder. He

leaned his shoulder against the soft padding and pushed as hard as he could.

He couldn't move it. Someone had snapped the padlock back into place. He was locked in! Jupe was trapped in the huge soundproofed building. No matter how loudly he called, no one outside would be able to hear him. There was no hope of his being rescued by chance either. No one in the studio would be trying to enter this sound stage until the first shift of workers showed up on Monday morning.

And in less than an hour and a half Bloodhound and Peggy and the others would begin taping the first of the Wee Rogues quiz shows.

Jupe stood absolutely still for a minute. His mind was racing, but not with panic. It was working in an orderly, methodical way. He was forming a plan, steps to be taken. One. Two. Three.

Step One. He needed light.

He remembered the evening before: Luther Lomax moving away from the master control panel after he had surprised the Three Investigators just as they were finding those silver cups.

Jupe groped his way carefully down the wall of the sound stage toward the far end where the kitchen set was. It seemed a long time before his reaching fingers touched the big metal switch box.

He found the catch and swung the front of it open. His hand brushed against a switch handle. He pulled it down.

The kitchen set was flooded with light.

Step Two. Phone.

It was only a few yards away from him, fastened to the wall. Jupe walked over to it and held the receiver to his ear.

The phone was dead.

7

TRAPPED!

Listening to the dead-silent receiver, the First Investigator wasn't discouraged. He hadn't really expected the phone to work. Whoever had locked him into the sound stage to keep him away from the quiz show would have had to make sure he couldn't phone for help.

Step Three. Fix it. If possible.

It was easy enough to find where the line had been cut, close to the floor. But whoever had cut it had done a thorough job. The wire hadn't simply been snipped through. A whole long section of it had been lifted out.

The carpenter's toolbox was still on the floor behind the kitchen set. There was a good strong pair of pliers in it. Finding a length of wire on a sound stage was no problem. Jupe took what he needed from a small, standing spotlight.

Working as fast as he could, he reconnected the two loose ends of the phone line. His heart was thumping as he lifted the receiver to his ear again. There was a faint but frightening possibility that the phone line had been cut outside the sound stage too.

Jupe listened to one of the sweetest sounds he had ever heard: the dial tone.

Jupe realized he could call the studio switch-board and ask them to send someone to let him out with a duplicate key. But it was easy to foresee all the questions and explanations he would have to go through if he did that. He decided this was a situation better kept between himself and the other two Investigators.

Pete had just come home from the beach. He answered the phone on the second ring. Jupe explained where he was and, as briefly as possible, what happened.

"Call Gordon Harker and ask him to drive you down here right away," he went on. "I'll try to cut through the padding at the bottom of the door so I can slip the key out to you."

Pete didn't waste a second after Jupe had hung up. He called the limo company and spoke to Gordon Harker. Within thirty minutes the chauffeur drew up outside Pete's house. Pete and Bob, who had ridden over on his bicycle in answer to Pete's urgent call, scrambled into the back of the car.

There was nothing the two Investigators could do now except sit back and try to relax as the limousine threaded its way quickly through the Saturday traffic toward Hollywood. At last it turned onto Vine Street. The studio gates came in sight.

Gordon Harker swung the car to a stop as the guard walked out of his booth and approached the limo.

"Let me see your pass, please," he said.

The two Investigators looked at each other. Both their faces were blank with dismay. They didn't have the studio pass. Jupiter had it.

The First Investigator gave a final tap to the chisel. Putting down his tools, he lifted away the thin sliver of wood he had cut from the bottom of the door and set it beside the strips of padding he had already hacked away. He lay down on the floor, keeping his eyes as close to the ground as he could.

It was okay. Step Four had been accomplished. He could see a thin line of light under the door now. As soon as Pete arrived, Jupe would be able to slip the key out to him.

Jupe looked at this watch. Seventeen minutes to two. What was keeping Pete? He should have been here by now. Had he had trouble getting through to the chauffeur? Or had something else held him up?

With a sense of unease, Jupiter Jones remembered his own puzzled suspicion of Gordon Harker.

The limousine was still stalled at the gate.

"We had a pass, but we left it at home," Pete told the guard. "Don't you remember us? We were here yesterday for the Wee Rogues' reunion. We've come to pick up our friend, Jupiter Jones."

The guard shook his head stolidly. "I don't know anything about that," he said. "There's no list of visitors for today. And I can't let you in without a pass."

"B-but . . ." Bob stammered helplessly. "But we've—"

He never got any further than that. Gordon Harker had opened the back door of the car.

"Okay, guys," he said. "You'd better spill out here."

Pete and Bob spilled out. Gordon Harker turned back to the guard.

"Limo for Milton Glass in publicity," he told him. "I just brought the kids along because they wanted to see the studio."

The guard nodded. "I don't think Mr. Glass is in his office—" he began.

"His secretary ordered the limo." The tall chauffeur cut him off before he could say any more. He closed the back door of the car. Pete was standing beside it. "Where is he?" Gordon Harker whispered to him.

"Stage Nine," Pete whispered back. "He's locked in. He'll pass you the key under the door."

The chauffeur slipped behind the wheel again. The guard waved him on. Pete and Bob watched the car disappear down the street of famous buildings.

Jupe was right, Bob thought. There *was* something mysterious about Gordon Harker.

Jupiter was still lying on the floor of the sound stage, watching the crack of light under the door. He saw it disappear.

"Pete?" Jupe called.

"No, it's me." The First Investigator could just hear the man's voice. "Your chauffeur, Gordon Harker. Pass me the key."

Jupe hesitated for an instant. After all the work he had done, fixing the phone, cutting away the padding and the wood of the door, he didn't want to give the key to the wrong person. To someone who might simply walk off and leave him there until Monday. It was even possible, he realized, that Harker had followed him to the studio earlier. That Harker was the one who had locked him in.

He glanced at his watch again. Twelve minutes to two. This was no time for hesitation. He had to take the chance that the chauffeur was on his side. He had to risk it.

He slipped the key though the crack under the door. He stood up. He waited.

The door opened.

Jupe stepped gratefully out into the bright sunlight.

"Thank you, Mr. Harker," he said.

"Better hurry," the chauffeur told him. "Your friends are at the gate. We'll pick them up, and I think we can just make it by two o'clock."

They did just make it. It was one minute to two when Jupe and the others ran into the big television network building and hurried to the elevators.

The doors of the studio on the seventeenth floor, where the quiz-show taping was scheduled to take place, were still open. A uniformed attendant hurried Jupe down the aisle and onto the stage.

He showed the First Investigator to his seat in a

long wooden stand like a jury box. While the attendant fastened a mike to his tie, Jupe looked carefully at Footsie, who was sitting next to him. He was watching Footsie's eyes.

"Hi," Footsie said. "Close thing."

He couldn't be absolutely sure, Jupe decided. You could never be certain about people's faces and reactions. But he would have staked his reputation as an investigator on it.

Footsie was not in the least surprised to see him there.

Jupe looked quickly at the other people on the stage. Peggy wasn't surprised either. She seemed relieved he had made it in time. She gave him a friendly, pleased smile.

Bloodhound looked pleased too. So did Milton Glass, who was hosting the quiz show.

The only one who did not meet Jupe's eyes when he looked at him, who glanced away uneasily, was the young man with the long blond hair down to his shoulders.

Bonehead.

8

THE FIRST QUIZ

The television cameras were rolling. The first "Wee Rogues Quiz Show" had begun.

After warming up the audience with his flashing smile and a few jokes, Milton Glass explained the rules of the quiz.

The contestants would answer questions in turn. Five points for a right answer, zero for a wrong one. If one of them missed a question, any of the others could hold up their hands and volunteer an answer, gaining five points if they came up with the right one. But if, after volunteering, they gave a wrong answer, they would *lose* five points.

Glass turned and beamed at the contestants. "So don't volunteer unless you're sure," he warned them.

He faced the cameras and the studio audience again.

"In some quiz shows," he continued, "there are several categories. The contestants can choose the one they think they know most about. But on this show there will be only one category. The Wee Rogues will be asked questions on only one subject"—he paused and his fine teeth sparkled again—"the Wee Rogues themselves."

There were excited murmurs among the audience.

Mr. Glass went on to explain. "In Sweden they have a saying, 'lying like an eyewitness.' Well, the Wee Rogues are going to be their own eyewitnesses. At the beginning of each program we're going to show them pieces of film edited out of their own Wee Rogues' comedies—outtakes. You in our studio audience will be able to watch the clips on this monitor."

He pointed to the large movie screen that had been set up on one side of the stage, facing the audience.

"And the contestants will watch them only once—on this one."

Jupe glanced at the screen facing him and Footsie and the others. He felt pretty good. If he had been able to choose any category in the world, he couldn't have thought of one better suited to his abilities than this one. With his exceptional memory and powers of observation, he didn't see how he could miss a single question. The thing to do, he decided, was to volunteer as often and as quickly as possible whenever anyone else came out with a wrong answer.

He looked at the contestants sitting beside him: Footsie and then Peggy, Bonehead, and Bloodhound. Only Bonehead was smiling.

"So on with the show," Milton Glass was saying. "Let's all watch the Wee Rogues and see what they're up to."

He took his seat at the desk under the electronic scoreboard. Jupe concentrated on the screen as the film began.

There was no story to it. It had been put together out of bits and pieces taken from several of the old comedies. The action kept cutting from one scene to another.

Bonehead and Bloodhound poured gunpowder into the flour that Pretty Peggy was using to make a cake. The black kid, Flapjack, with his spiky hair like a porcupine's quills, let the air out of the tires of Footsie's bicycle. A middle-aged stranger, played by a character actor who had appeared now and then in the series, gave the Wee Rogues a dollar to watch his car, which was full of stolen radios. Baby Fatso was kidnapped and tied to a tree by the other kids, who were planning to ransom him for a box of candy bars. Bonehead, the drooping lobes of his ears wiggling with mischief, persuaded Flapjack to dig for buried treasure in a patch of poison ivy while the others watched and giggled. Pretty Peggy rescued Baby Fatso, untying the knots that bound him to the tree. . . .

After exactly two minutes the film came to an end. The lights on the stage and in the audience were turned up again. The audience, who had been laughing appreciatively while the film was being shown, clapped and then settled down. The cameras moved in on Milton Glass as he swiveled around in his chair to face the competitors.

Peggy was given the first question.

"Who let the air out of the tires of a motorbike?" Glass asked her with his most disarming smile.

"No one." Peggy didn't smile back. Jupe was struck by her frowning determination. It obviously meant a lot to her to win the quiz. He remembered what she had said about needing money to put herself through college.

"It wasn't a motorbike," she went on. "It was an

ordinary bicycle, and it was Flapjack who deflated the tires."

"Right." The audience applauded. Milton Glass rang up five points for Peggy on the electronic scoreboard.

Bonehead was next. He was asked what color the bicycle was, and he got it right without a second's hesitation.

"Green."

Again the audience clapped.

It was Bloodhound's turn.

"What side of the handlebars was the three-speed gear on?"

Bloodhound hesitated. "On the right?" he suggested doubtfully.

A dismayed murmur came from the onlookers. Jupe's hand shot up an instant before Bonehead's. He waited while Milton Glass told Bloodhound how sorry he was that he had come up with the wrong answer.

"We've got two volunteers to answer that question," Glass went on, beaming at both of them. Then he pointed to Jupe.

"It didn't have a three-speed gear," the First Investigator told him in his puzzled, playing-it-dumb voice.

"Right."

A big burst of applause. And five more points for Jupe. Bonehead was scowling as the points were rung up on the scoreboard.

Footsie's turn.

The question was an easy one. "What was the extra ingredient in Pretty Peggy's cake?"

"Gunpowder."

"Right."

Five points and polite clapping for Footsie.

Milton Glass turned his smile on Jupiter Jones.

"How many knots did Pretty Peggy have to untie to release Baby Fatso from the tree?"

Jupe saw Peggy's hand go up before he even had time to pretend to be puzzled. He was almost tempted to get the answer wrong so she could win another five points, but he couldn't afford to let Bonehead get ahead of him on Bonehead's next turn.

"Four kn-n-nots?" Jupe said, making it sound like a lucky guess.

"Right."

Another round of applause marked the end of the first segment. Milton Glass laboriously read out the scores, although everyone could see them as clearly as he could. He obviously enjoyed being on camera.

Jupe looked out over the audience to the control

room at the back, where Luther Lomax was watching his monitoring screens. The elderly director looked as tense as a pilot trying to land a plane in a heavy fog.

Shifting his gaze, the First Investigator spotted Bob and Pete in the fifth row of the audience. They were sitting beside Gordon Harker. The chauffeur had a clipboard on his lap and was jotting on it with a pen.

Pete raised his clasped hands in a prizefighter's signal of victory when he saw Jupe looking at him.

Bob was sitting next to Harker. He couldn't help glancing at the clipboard the chauffeur was holding. Harker smiled and showed him what he had written on it.

Ordinary bicycle.

Green.

No three-speed gear.

Gunpowder.

Four.

"I was just trying to guess the answers before the contestants," he explained. "I'm doing pretty well so far. Got every one right." He pointed to the check marks he had made beside each line.

The next round of questions began. Peggy and Bonehead came up with the right answers. Bloodhound goofed again and Bonehead volunteered a split second ahead of Jupe and gave the right answer. Footsie muffed it too this time and Jupe had his hand up before Bonehead or Peggy and won himself another five points.

Milton Glass went into his score-reading routine after each round, hogging the attention of the cameras with his brilliant smile and charming the audience with a few more jokes.

By the beginning of the fifth and final round, Jupe was still five points ahead of Bonehead and ten points ahead of Peggy. Bloodhound and Footsie were both well out of the race.

The last round of questions began.

"What was suspicious about the stranger's car?" Milton Glass asked Peggy.

"It was full of stolen radios."

"Right. Five points for Pretty Peggy."

Applause from the audience.

Bonehead won himself another five points too by identifying the make of the car and even coming up with the right year. It was an antique. A Pierce-Arrow '29.

This time Bloodhound got an easy one.

"How much money did the stranger give the Wee Rogues to keep an eye on his car?"

"A dollar."

"Right."

More applause.

Even Footsie won on this round. He remembered the nickname the Wee Rogues had given to the stranger. They had called him Mr. Trouble.

It was Jupe's turn, the last question of the first quiz show.

"What was the name of the actor who played Mr. Trouble?"

It wasn't strictly fair of the quiz master to ask Jupe that. It had nothing to do with the film they had been shown, so it wasn't an eyewitness question. Unless Jupe could remember the name of an actor he had met only a few times when he was three years old, he would lose five points.

Bonehead and Peggy were both frantically waving their hands.

Jupe scratched his head in a puzzled way. He was only pretending not to know, still playing it dumb to confuse Bonehead. He had happened to run into the aging character actor some time before when the Three Investigators were working on a museum robbery, and had recognized him at once and remembered his name then.

"Edmund F-F-Frank," he said with his dumbest smile.

"Right."

The audience went wild.

The show was over. Jupe was still five points ahead of Bonehead. The audience filed out. Milton Glass reminded the contestants to be back at the TV station at two o'clock sharp the next afternoon.

Frowning, Peggy hurried away. Jupe watched her go. He felt sorry for her and wished there was something he could do to help her. But as long as Bonehead was his closest competitor, Jupe was determined to go on winning. He felt he still had a score to settle with Bonehead for the way the child actor had treated him years ago.

Jupe started across the stage to join the other two Investigators in the empty auditorium. A long leather sleeve shot out. Bonehead grabbed him roughly by the arm. His grip was like steel.

"Watch it, Baby Fatso," the tall young man snarled. "I'm onto you. I know all about you and your Three Investigators. You're playing dumb so you'll win the twenty thousand."

Jupiter turned. Bonehead gripped his arm even tighter.

"I'm warning you, Fatso," his persecutor said. "Cut it out. Or else." He walked away.

Bob and Pete were waiting for Jupe in the aisle. Gordon Harker had gone to get the limousine.

"What was Bonehead saying to you?" Pete asked Jupe.

The First Investigator didn't answer. He had a question of his own.

"Bob," he said. "You were sitting next to Gordon Harker, weren't you?"

"Sure. Why?"

"What was he writing on that clipboard all the way through the show?"

"Nothing much." Bob shrugged. "He was just trying to guess the answers to the questions before you did."

"Did you see his answers?" Jupe was frowning. His voice had that probing sound that meant he was onto some clue and intended to follow it up until he saw where it led.

"Sure. He showed them to me. He was doing fine. He got them all right except one."

"Which one?" the First Investigator asked eagerly. "That last one about Edmund Frank? Did he get that one wrong?"

"No." Bob shook his head. "The only one he missed was the make of Mr. Trouble's car. He had Edmund Frank written down long before you came up with it."

Jupe stared at him, then nodded and started up the aisle. Although Bob and Pete tried to question him as they all went down in the elevator, he refused to tell them why he was so interested in the chauffeur's answers to the questions in the quiz.

It wasn't until all three were out on the sidewalk waiting for the limousine that the First Investigator spoke again.

"I can understand his getting all those other questions right," Jupe said thoughtfully. "Because he saw the film too and he's obviously an intelligent man. But what beats me . . ." His voice trailed off.

"What?" the other two Investigators pressed him. "Go on, Jupe, tell us. What's the mystery?"

"The mystery is," the First Investigator said in a faraway voice, "the mystery is why a limousine chauffeur is so interested in the Wee Rogues."

9

THE MAN WHO
KNEW TOO MUCH

"Possible suspects," Jupiter Jones said. "Number One." He held up a stubby finger. "Footsie."

The Three Investigators were sitting in Headquarters. They had gone there straight from the television station. Jupe was behind the desk. Bob and Pete were in their usual places.

"Footsie," the First Investigator repeated. "What do we know about him?"

He didn't expect an answer. He was thinking aloud, as he often did when something puzzled him.

"We know he could have stolen those silver cups," he went on. "But then so could any of the other Rogues. We were all standing around that buffet table. There was a crowd of people on that kitchen set—waiters, electricians, grips. Any one of us could have slipped around the back to where the cups were. Any one of us could have been gone for two or three minutes without anybody noticing it."

"Bonehead," Pete suggested, leaning back in his rocking chair. "That's my hunch."

Jupe held up his hand in a way that meant wait a second. "Let's concentrate on Footsie first," he said. "The director, Luther Lomax, suspects Footsie. He saw him hanging around Stage Nine later that night. He thought Footsie had come back to retrieve the stolen cups. Lomax scared him away. But he was sure Footsie would try again. And maybe he was right. At eleven forty-five this morning Footsie jumps on his motorbike and heads for the movie studio. I go after him. I get there first. Footsie sees me enter the sound stage. He panics. He locks me in . . ."

"Makes sense," Bob agreed.

"Maybe." Jupe pinched his lip. It might make sense, he thought, but it left a lot of loose ends. Because it seemed to Jupe that whoever had locked him in the sound stage had done it, not out of panic, but for a very good reason. To keep him away from the quiz show. To knock him out as a competitor. And Footsie had never seemed to care about the quiz. He had obviously never thought he had a chance of winning anyway.

On the other hand, Jupe didn't believe in coincidences. He didn't believe it was a coincidence that Footsie had just happened to be going to the movie studio on his motorbike that morning.

"Suspect Number Two." The First Investigator held up a second stubby finger.

"Bonehead," Pete put in eagerly.

"Bonehead," Jupe agreed. "He's smart. He's greedy for money. He despises Milton Glass and the whole idea of the Rogues' reunion. He insists on getting paid a hundred dollars just to appear on the talk show. He's determined to win the quiz. He suspects my dumb-kid act and finds out my background."

"How do you know that?" Bob interrupted.

"That's what Bonehead was telling me when he grabbed my arm right after the show today," Jupe said absently. "Where was I? Oh, so if Bonehead saw me walk into Stage Nine an hour and a half before the taping started, he might seize the chance to get rid of a dangerous competitor. And when I do arrive at the television station just in time, Bonehead is the only one who looks surprised to see me."

He remembered the way Bonehead had glanced away uneasily at the sight of him joining the other contestants.

"But then what was Bonehead doing at the movie studio this morning?" the First Investigator asked. "At the same time as Footsie?"

"He could have just happened to be there, couldn't he?" Bob suggested.

"No." Jupe shook his head firmly, and this time he said it aloud. "I don't believe in coincidences."

He was silent for a moment, thinking, before he held up a third stubby finger.

"Suspect Number Three. Gordon Harker."

"I don't think he stole those cups." Bob had grown to like their chauffeur. "He just isn't the type."

"Maybe, maybe not." Jupe privately agreed with Records, but he wasn't going to rule out Harker just because he seemed like such a nice guy.

"He was there on the sound stage yesterday," he pointed out. "I saw him right at the beginning of the talk show. He was walking around toward the back of the set where the cups and the unused arc lights were. He's taken a strange interest in this Wee Rogues' reunion ever since it started. He asks me for a ticket to the quiz. He sits there with a clip-board trying to guess the answers and writing them down. He knows the name of an obscure character actor in the series. But at the same time he's rather shy about his interest. He claims he doesn't know where Stage Nine is. . . ." Jupe's voice trailed off. He looked at his two friends.

"You might say," he went on after a minute, "that Gordon Harker is not only the man who knows too little. Like the title of that old Hitchcock movie, he's also the man who knows too much."

Glancing at his watch, Pete jumped to his feet. "It's four o'clock, Jupe," he said.

Jupe hesitated and glanced at the television set. It was the scheduled time for another of the *Wee Rogues* comedies to be televised by the network. It would be agony for him to have to watch it, to see himself playing Baby Fatso. On the other hand, it might help him on the quiz tomorrow. As a contestant it was part of his homework to study every foot of film he could.

"Okay," he said, sighing. "Turn it on, Bob."

The first commercial had just come to an end. Jupe winced as Baby Fatso appeared on the screen.

"Pleath let me come," Baby Fatso pleaded.

The other Wee Rogues all shook their heads. They were going into town to buy some ice cream, and they didn't want to be bothered taking the baby with them.

"But we can't just leave him here," Pretty Peggy said. "Poor little thing."

"Okay, you stay with him," Bonehead told her.

But Peggy wanted to go into town too. In the end they decided to draw lots for it.

"Yeah, lotth and lotth," Baby Fatso said. "Lotth and lotth of ice cream."

Bonehead cheated and Flapjack lost.

"How come Ah gets to do all the chores around here?" the black kid moaned in his singsong voice. "Ah ain't cut out to be no baby-sitter."

The episode was the one about Mr. Trouble and his carful of stolen radios. Mr. Trouble paid the Wee Rogues to watch the car while he made a phone call. They were all horsing around in the old Pierce-Arrow convertible when the police arrived. The kids were hauled off to the police station.

Back in the kitchen Flapjack decided to make his own ice cream. Baby Fatso helped him, putting salt in it instead of sugar.

Mr. Trouble stole his convertible back from the police. There was a car chase, the Wee Rogues whooping and yelling in the back of the police car. . . .

Jupe stood up and turned the set off.

"But how did it come out?" Pete protested. "Did they catch Mr. Trouble?"

"No," Jupe told him. "They wanted to use the same actor, Edmund Frank, in a later episode in which he hired Flapjack to steal a dog for him, so they let him get away that time."

He picked up the phone and dialed a number. "Hullo, Mr. Harker," he said after a moment. "It's Jupiter Jones here. I wonder if you'd mind coming out to the salvage yard. Yes, as soon as possible."

"Where are we going?" Bob wanted to know after Jupe had hung up.

"Nowhere," Jupe answered in his thinking-aloud voice. "It just occurred to me that if we're going to find out who did steal those cups we need an ally, a friend. Someone whom nobody suspects."

He refused to say any more until the limousine pulled up at the gates. Uncle Titus and Aunt Mathilda had gone to an auction. Jupe invited Gordon Harker into the house across the street from the salvage yard to have a cup of coffee.

They all sat in the large, pleasant kitchen. Jupe put a pot of coffee on the stove for Mr. Harker and got sodas for the Three Investigators.

Jupiter started to talk about the quiz show. "I'm glad they didn't ask me what make that car was," he said. "I didn't know the answer to that question either."

"Didn't you?" Gordon Harker sipped his coffee. "You knew all the other answers."

"Yes, but I was never in any of those scenes," Jupe explained. "The scenes with Mr. Trouble's convertible. Bonehead and Bloodhound and the others were, and I guess they must have asked Luther Lomax or someone what kind of car it was then. That's how Bonehead knew. He remembered it was a Pierce-Arrow. But I never even saw the car."

"Yeah, that's right," the chauffeur agreed. "I was watching that episode on television just before you called." He smiled. "You and that black kid, Flapjack, stayed home and made your own ice cream."

"Do you like watching those old shows?" Jupe asked.

Harker shrugged. "They're kind of silly," he admitted. "But they give me a laugh sometimes."

"They are pretty silly." Jupe nodded. "But that was the whole point, wasn't it? They made us all act like idiots. Bonehead with his wiggling ears. Bloodhound with his lolling tongue. Me with my lisp. Footsie with his enormous feet. And Flapjack with his singsong way of talking."

Jupe paused for a moment.

"How come Ah gets to do all the chores around here?" Jupe was giving an excellent imitation of the black kid's voice. "Ah ain't cut out to be no baby-sitter."

Gordon Harker laughed. "That's pretty good," he said.

The First Investigator leaned forward across the table.

"It all seems rather embarrassing now, doesn't it?" he asked. "At least it does to me."

"I guess it must." The chauffeur picked up his cap. "Well, let's get going," he suggested. "Where do you want me to drive you?"

"Nowhere, right now." Jupe held out his hand. "I just wanted to say hello."

Bob and Pete stared at him. What was Jupe up to? What was he talking about?

Jupe was still holding his hand out. He waited until the chauffeur shook it.

"It's good to see you again, Flapjack," the First Investigator said.

10

RENDEZVOUS IN HOLLYWOOD

"Well," Gordon Harker said, "I guess I was luckier than most of the other Wee Rogues, except Bone-head maybe. I never used my own name as an actor and when the series folded I had no trouble at school. With my hair combed out—instead of twisted up into those awful spikes—and my natural voice, no one recognized me as Flapjack."

He finished his coffee and Jupe poured him another cup. The other two Investigators waited eagerly for the chauffeur to continue with his story.

"My parents had saved my movie earnings for me," he went on. "I was a good student, and when I finished high school at sixteen, I was able to go on to teacher's college and become a teacher."

He looked across the table at Jupe. "I'm still a

teacher," he said. "I like it. I like the job. I like the kids I work with. The school's in what you might call a pretty tough neighborhood, and they're a rough bunch, those kids. But they don't give me any trouble. I get along with them fine."

He smiled wryly. "When the network started running those *Wee Rogues* comedies," he said, "it scared me to death for a while. If those tough kids in my classes ever found out I was Flapjack, my life wouldn't be worth living. Can you imagine how they'd make fun of me? 'How come Ah gets to do all the chores around here?' " He imitated Flapjack's singsong voice. "I couldn't walk into the school without them kidding me, yelling stuff like that at me."

Jupiter nodded sympathetically. He remembered those last three weeks before summer vacation, the boys and girls in his own school coming up to him in the yard. "Say 'Pleath thtop,' Baby Fatso. Pleath."

"And yet," Gordon Harker went on in a puzzled way, "I couldn't help remembering the old days. And I was sort of fascinated, wondering what had happened to the other Wee Rogues. How they'd all made out. I'd been earning some extra money working for the Easy-Ride Limo Company for a couple of years during vacation time. I'd even had some assignments driving for the old movie studio. And when I read about the Wee Rogues' reunion, I just couldn't seem to stay away from it. I swapped jobs with one of the other drivers so I could be around the studio during the reunion. So I could check up on the old Rogues and see what they were all like now."

"If you drove for the studio often," Jupe said, "why did you have to ask directions to Stage Nine?"

"Oh, it's a huge lot," Mr. Harker said. "And I'd never been called to that particular sound stage since I was a kid. I never really paid attention to directions when my parents drove me to shootings. I was too busy memorizing my lines and trying to stay awake."

He stirred sugar into his coffee and then looked across at Jupe again.

"Of course, I didn't think anyone would ever recognize me," he said. "I never thought anyone would guess I was Flapjack. Because as far as Milton Glass and the studio could tell, Flapjack had just disappeared when the series ended. No one knew where he was or what had become of him. They couldn't trace him."

He sipped his coffee and put his cup down. "I

guess I just didn't count on your being so smart," he told Jupe.

"I wasn't so smart." Jupe glanced down modestly at his soda can. "It was mostly luck, and Bob seeing your answers to those questions."

Privately, the First Investigator felt he was stretching the truth a little. He didn't really think luck had had anything to do with it. It was his own remarkable deductive powers that had identified Gordon Harker as Flapjack.

He had put all the clues together—the fact that Harker hadn't been able to identify Mr. Trouble's car as a Pierce-Arrow because Flapjack had never been in any of those car scenes. The fact that Mr. Harker *had* known the name of Edmund Frank, the actor who had played Mr. Trouble, because in a later episode Mr. Trouble hired Flapjack to steal a dog for him. So the two of them spent several days working together.

Jupe had figured it all out and come up with the logical and correct solution.

"Do you mind answering a question?" Jupiter said.

"Shoot," said Mr. Harker.

"When I was sitting in the sound stage during the taping of the talk show, I noticed you walking toward a group of arc lights behind the set. What were you doing?"

"Ah," chuckled the chauffeur. "You caught me. I've always been curious about the technical aspects of show business—even when I played Flapjack. There was a chance for me to get close to the lighting and see how it was rigged."

"That explains it," Jupiter said, smiling. "And it also explains why an investigator should never make assumptions not based on facts. For a while I suspected that you were the one who stashed the stolen loving cups in that arc light."

"Innocent on all counts," said Mr. Harker. "What are you going to do now? Are you going to give me away, tell everyone who I am?"

"Of course not." Jupe looked at the other two Investigators. "None of us are going to say a word about it to anybody, are we?"

"No way," Pete assured him. "Not a single word."

"No," Bob agreed. "Your secret's safe with us, Mr. Harker."

Gordon Harker let out his breath in a long sigh. "Thanks," he said. "That makes me feel a lot better."

There was a silence.

"But we did hope," Jupe said after a moment. "I mean, you don't have to. But we wondered if you'd be willing to help us, Mr. Harker."

"Sure. If I can," Gordon Harker told him. "What do you want me to do?"

Jupe explained about the stolen silver cups, about Luther Lomax engaging them to find the thief. He took one of the Three Investigators cards from his pocket and showed it to Harker.

"You see," he said, "when we're on a case like this—even though we've already found those cups—well, we can't give up until we've solved the whole mystery. We have to find out who stole the cups. That's the way the Three Investigators work. We've never left a case unsolved."

Harker nodded. He seemed to understand that.

"How can I help you?" he asked.

"It seems to me we've got two main suspects," Jupe told him. "Bonehead and Footsie." He had been thinking about that while waiting for the chauffeur and had come up with an idea that seemed to rule out those coincidences he disliked so much.

"Let's suppose they pulled off the cup theft together," he suggested. "That way, everything begins to make more sense. Bonehead and Footsie agreed to meet at the movie studio today at noon. As far as they knew, those stolen cups were still hidden in that arc light and they wanted to get them. Bonehead was outside the sound stage waiting for Footsie. He saw me go in. It gave him an idea. Winning that twenty thousand dollars was much more important to him than those cups. So he locked me in Stage Nine to keep me away from the quiz show. When Footsie showed up on his motorbike, Bonehead simply told him the sound stage was padlocked, they'd have to try again some other time."

"So Footsie wasn't surprised to see you show up in time for the quiz," Pete put in.

"But Bonehead was," Bob agreed.

"Right." Jupe looked at Gordon Harker. "That's where we need your help," he said.

"Okay. As a teacher I enjoy solving problems as much as you do." The tall young man finished his coffee. "But you still haven't told me what you want me to do."

"We want to tail them," Jupe explained. "See if they get together again. See if they go back to that sound stage this evening."

"Okay." Gordon Harker stood up. "Where do we start?"

"That's the whole point." Jupe stayed in his seat, looking up at Harker. "That's where we need your help first. We don't know where either Bonehead or Footsie is living. So we don't have a place to start unless we can get their addresses."

"I don't know." Harker shook his head. "Neither of them was assigned a limo. Because they both have their own transportation. Bonehead has a little British open sports job. And Footsie has that motorbike. So the office of Easy-Ride Limos wouldn't have their addresses either."

"But the guard at the studio gate does," Jupe reminded him. "At least he had my address when I checked in for the lunch yesterday. So he probably has Bonehead's and Footsie's too. But I don't think he'd give them to *us* if we asked him."

"He wouldn't even let Pete and me in the gate this afternoon," Bob remembered.

The chauffeur thought that over for a moment.

"I could try," he said. "The limo company does a lot of business with the studio. I could say I had a call to collect all the Wee Rogues for a special meeting."

He picked up his cap and put it on.

"Let's see how I make out," he suggested. "Come on."

He let the Three Investigators off a block from the studio gates on Vine Street and then drove on to talk to the guard.

Jupe and his two friends went into a drugstore to have a quick hamburger while they waited for him. They didn't have long to wait. Jupe could see at once from Gordon Harker's smile when he walked in that he had got what they wanted.

He had all the Rogues' addresses written on a sheet of paper. The Three Investigators studied it while they were munching their supper at the drugstore counter. Peggy was staying in a hotel in Santa Monica. Bloodhound lived at home with his father in Beverly Hills. Bonehead and Footsie had apartments in Hollywood.

"Let's try Bonehead first," Jupe decided.

"After I finish this," Pete objected.

So once the boys' plates were clean and Mr. Harker had had a sandwich, they all piled into the limousine again.

Bonehead's address was the Magnolia Arms on a street called Las Palmas, not far from Hollywood Boulevard. It was more like a motel than an apartment house. Inside a narrow archway two lines of small wooden cabins faced each other across a courtyard. Next to the complex was a small parking lot.

Gordon Harker parked the limousine on the street while the Three Investigators crept into the court. It was dark now. Only a few of the cabins showed any lights in their windows.

They were in luck. According to Gordon Harker's list, Bonehead's apartment was number 10. Although the curtains were drawn in that cabin at the far end of the court, Jupe could see a glow through them. Bonehead was probably home.

The First Investigator motioned to his two friends and they walked silently on the grass down the court. There was a large magnolia bush directly facing the door of number 10. The three friends squatted in the darkness beneath it, watching the door of Bonehead's cabin.

The top of the door was made of glass. Venetian blinds were lowered over it, but Jupe could see that some of the slats were worn and bent. If someone could press his face against the glass, he would be able to see into the apartment.

"This looks like a job for you," Jupe whispered to Pete.

Pete sighed. He had heard those words from Jupe before, on other cases. They meant there was something difficult and usually dangerous to be done, something that required Pete's special skills.

The Second Investigator was by far the most athletic of the three. He could run faster than either Jupe or Bob; he could move stealthily, silently, on the balls of his feet.

"Okay," he whispered back after a moment. "I'll see what I can see."

Crouching, he started forward away from the sheltering darkness of the magnolia bush, across the strip of grass that separated him from Bonehead's cabin.

He had gone only a few steps when he dropped face down onto the ground, pressing into the earth as though trying to sink into it.

The door of Bonehead's apartment had opened.

Jupe saw the tall young man in his leather jacket silhouetted against the light.

Any moment, Pete thought, and Bonehead was sure to spot him, lying there only a few yards away.

He remembered the violent way Bonehead had grabbed Jupe's arm after the quiz show that afternoon. If he found the Three Investigators spying on him he would be very angry and probably dangerous.

Bonehead turned his head and looked back into the lighted room behind him.

"Come on," he said impatiently, pulling a comb down through his long hair. "Let's go. It's time."

The First Investigator clenched his fists. It would

be bad enough to have to face Bonehead alone. If Footsie was there too, the Three Investigators didn't stand a chance.

He wished Gordon Harker were with them. But the chauffeur wasn't in sight, not even within calling distance. He was sitting in the parked limousine across the street from the courtyard.

Bonehead lifted his hand, reaching inside the doorway. A figure in blue jeans and a denim shirt appeared beside him. Then Bonehead's groping fingers found the switch. The lights in the cabin went off.

Bonehead slammed the cabin door shut. The two figures moved forward in the almost total darkness.

Pete didn't dare raise his head to look at them. He lay without moving, pressed down into the grass. He didn't even see their feet as they passed within a few inches of him, but he felt as though they were treading on him.

In that instant before Bonehead turned off the light and the two figures stepped away from the door, Jupiter had seen them both quite clearly. He had had time to recognize Bonehead's companion.

It was Peggy.

Jupe stood watching her back as she and Bonehead walked toward the archway and disappeared into the street.

Pete joined him. "It was pure blind luck they didn't trip over me," he said, sounding a little breathless, as he often did after a narrow escape. If there was one thing the Second Investigator didn't enjoy, it was taking risks.

But the First Investigator was already hurrying after Bonehead and Peggy. Bob and Pete fell in behind him.

By the time they reached the archway the young man in the leather jacket and the young woman in jeans were twenty yards away, walking quickly along the sidewalk toward Hollywood Boulevard. Gordon Harker was parked across the street, the limousine pointing in the opposite direction. He would have to make a U-turn to catch up with Bonehead and Peggy. Jupe made a quick decision.

"Ask Mr. Harker to swing around," he told Pete. "And follow me, back me up. Come on, Bob, we'll try to keep them in sight."

Pete ran across the street to the limousine. Jupe and Bob hurried along the sidewalk toward the boulevard.

There were a few pedestrians on Las Palmas. If Bonehead looked back, he might catch sight of the two Investigators following him. Jupe and Bob kept their distance, staying close to the storefronts.

After a minute Jupe heard the limousine coming

up behind him. He was within fifteen yards of Hollywood Boulevard by then. He saw Bonehead and
Peggy pause at the traffic light there. He waited
until the limousine pulled up beside him. He
opened the back door to climb in.

And then everything happened very quickly.

Bonehead and Peggy crossed Hollywood Boulevard.

Bob and Jupe jumped into the limousine.

A yellow foreign car appeared for a moment at
the corner of the boulevard.

The limousine glided quickly forward.

Jupe leaned out of the window to keep his eyes
on Bonehead and Peggy.

They had disappeared.

The yellow car sped across the intersection.

"Go after it," Jupe said.

Gordon Harker went after it. But the lights
changed to red. There was no way the chauffeur
could make a left turn to follow the foreign car.
Jupe caught a glimpse of two familiar figures sitting
in the back of it as it raced out of sight down Hollywood Boulevard.

Bonehead and Peggy.

Gordon Harker took off his cap and relaxed behind the wheel, waiting for the lights to change
again.

"Sorry," he said. "I'm afraid we've lost them."

"It's not your fault," Jupe reassured him. He knew exactly what had happened. Bonehead and Peggy had arranged to meet the yellow car at the intersection of Las Palmas and the boulevard. That was how they had disappeared. They had simply jumped into the back of the car the moment the lights changed.

"It doesn't matter," Jupe went on thoughtfully. "At least we've learned something."

"You mean about Peggy?" Bob asked. "About her being with Bonehead?"

Jupiter nodded. "And something that might be even more important than that," he said. "We've all seen that big fancy yellow foreign car before. We know who it belongs to."

"We do?" Pete said.

"Who?" Bob asked.

"The head of publicity at the movie studio," the First Investigator told them. "Milton Glass."

11

A LUCKY WIND

The First Investigator got up early the next morning. He helped himself to some cereal and a glass of milk in the empty kitchen, then went out to his workshop.

It was a windy day. He had to rig a tarpaulin around his bench before he could start work.

Although he had no immediate use in mind yet for his new invention, a special investigator's camera, he was glad to keep working on it. Puttering helped him think.

As he assembled the tiny pieces of metal and fitted them together, his brain was busy assembling the pieces of the puzzle of the stolen silver cups.

There were several pieces of that puzzle that just didn't fit, Jupe was thinking. He still thought it possible that when Footsie had chugged off on his old motorbike heading for the studio the day before, he had been going to meet Bonehead to retrieve the stolen cups from the sound stage.

But what had Footsie been doing at the television network building in the first place? He had walked in off the street two hours before taping time. He had ridden up in the elevator, but not to the seventeenth floor where the quiz studio was. Then five minutes later he had appeared in the lobby again.

What had he been doing during those five minutes? Visiting someone in an office?

Who?

And Milton Glass. Why had he picked up Peggy and Bonehead on the corner of Hollywood Boulevard the night before?

If he had just wanted to take them out to dinner or something—and remembering the hostility between Bonehead and Glass, Jupe didn't think that was very likely anyway—why hadn't he simply driven up to the Magnolia Arms and picked them up there?

That whole rendezvous on Hollywood Boulevard reminded Jupe of a scene in a spy film. It had all been done so quickly, so secretively. A clandestine operation, as it's always called in those movies.

Within three hours Jupe had the camera finished.

It was in a metal case almost as thin as a pocket comb and not much wider. Jupe slipped it behind the lapel of his jacket. It made no bulge that anyone would ever notice. He was pushing the slightly protruding lens through his buttonhole when he saw the light above the workbench flashing.

Thirty seconds later he had wriggled through Tunnel Two, pushed his way through the trapdoor, and snatched up the phone.

"Jupiter Jones speaking," he said.

"Hello. I'm glad I found you home." The voice was so friendly and cordial you could hear the smile in it.

"Mr. Glass?" Jupe asked.

"Let's just say I'm a friend," the cordial voice told him. "A friend of Pretty Peggy's. And I wouldn't want her to have an accident, would you?"

"Of course not," Jupe said. "But why should she have an accident? Where is she?"

"Never mind where she is, Baby Fatso." The voice still sounded full of smiles. "She's quite safe at the moment. I just wanted to warn you, she won't be safe much longer." There was a brief pause. "Not if you win that quiz today, Baby Fatso. If you do, Pretty Peggy's going to end up in the hospital, and she'll be there a long time."

"Wait a—" Jupe began. But there was no point in saying anything more. He heard a click and then a dial tone.

Jupe hung up and sat down beside his desk.

He had the list of addresses Gordon Harker had given him in his pocket. He picked up the phone again and dialed the number of Peggy's hotel in Santa Monica.

The desk clerk answered and rang Peggy's room.

"She's not in," he reported a minute later.

"Did she check out?" Jupe asked.

No, she hadn't checked out. But now that the desk clerk came to think of it, he hadn't seen her at all that morning, although her key was in its box.

Jupe thanked him and replaced the receiver. He sat perfectly still for a few minutes, frowning and pinching his lip. At the end of those few minutes he shook his head several times.

"That wasn't Milton Glass who called," he said softly to himself.

For one thing he didn't believe Milton Glass would have called him Baby Fatso. He had never used that hated name. He called him Jupiter or Jupe. So, if it wasn't Milton Glass threatening Peggy on the phone, it was a very good actor imitating Glass's voice.

Who? Bonehead? But Bonehead had always been

the worst actor of all the Wee Rogues. Most of the time he couldn't even remember his lines. And when he did remember them, he could never speak them as though he meant them. His only talent had been wiggling his big ears.

The wind was whistling around the old mobile home hidden behind its pile of junk.

And Bonehead had an open sports car. It gave Jupe an idea. He picked up the phone once more and called Gordon Harker. He arranged with the chauffeur to collect Pete and Bob and bring them to the salvage yard as quickly as he could.

After Jupe had hung up, he sat for a few more minutes behind his desk. With the plan that had formed in his mind, he would have a use for that secret investigator's camera sooner than he had expected.

There was a tiny darkroom inside Headquarters. Jupe went into it and loaded the camera with film. It had been impossible to fit spools into the flat case. The one flaw in Jupe's new invention was that it was only equipped to take a single exposure before the film had to be changed.

But a single exposure would be enough if the First Investigator's hunch was correct and he timed it just right.

He slipped the camera back under his lapel and

adjusted the lens in his buttonhole. It hardly showed, a small circle of glass surrounded by a brass star that could easily have been mistaken for a badge.

He didn't have to wait long for Pete and Bob at the gate.

"Some wind," Bob said as Jupe climbed into the back of the limousine.

"Yes," he agreed. "A lucky wind. At least I hope it will be."

He didn't explain what he meant by that. He didn't say anything else until Gordon Harker parked the limousine across the street from the Magnolia Arms.

"You go, Pete," he said then.

"Oh, no," the Second Investigator protested. "Not another special job for me."

Jupe smiled. "All you have to do is look in the parking lot," he said. "See if Bonehead's sports car is there."

Pete was back in three minutes.

"Yep," he said. "It's there all right. A little red job."

Jupe leaned forward in his seat. "Is the top down?" he asked.

"Yep. One of those canvas things."

Jupe nodded, pleased. "Let's hope it stays

down," he said. "Then it really could be a lucky wind."

He glanced at his watch. Not quite half past twelve. There was no telling how long they might have to wait before Bonehead left for the television studio, and he didn't want to wait in the limousine, parked directly across from the archway in front of the apartments. Bonehead was sure to notice the long black car as soon as he stepped out onto the sidewalk.

Ten yards away was the entrance to a narrow cross street running into Las Palmas.

"Could you park down there?" he asked Gordon Harker. "Facing Las Palmas? Then whichever way he turns when he comes out of the parking lot, we'll be able to follow him."

"Sure," the chauffeur agreed. "Good idea."

He drove the limousine forward, then backed into the cross street, pulling far enough back from Las Palmas not to be noticeable from the courtyard.

Jupe checked his camera, then sat back to wait.

It was just after one o'clock when the Three Investigators saw Bonehead walk out through the archway and head for the parking lot. Gordon Harker switched on the ignition. By the time Bonehead's little red sports car pulled out onto Las Palmas and made a right turn toward Hollywood

Boulevard, the limousine was already gliding forward.

Harker went after Bonehead.

Bonehead made another right turn on the boulevard. He was obviously going to the television studio.

"Keep a little behind him," Jupe advised the chauffeur. "Then when I say 'Now,' speed up and come up beside him. Get me as close to him as you can."

The First Investigator was sitting on the right-hand side in the backseat. Looking through the windshield, he could see the red sports car with Bonehead at the wheel. His long blond hair was streaming back from his head. Jupe leaned forward. With only a single exposure in his camera, he would have just one chance to get the picture he wanted.

Both cars went through a green light. There was a long, fairly empty stretch of the boulevard in front of them. Bonehead was increasing speed. In the open car with the wind in his face, his blond hair was whipped back even farther. His cheeks and his neck were visible all the way up to his scalp.

Watching him, the First Investigator felt a surge of excitement.

"Now," he said.

The limousine shot forward. It drew abreast of the sports car. Jupe swiveled in his seat, facing the window beside him. He pressed his lapel close to the glass.

If Bonehead turned his head now and glanced at the limousine, Jupe's one chance would be lost. His plan would be ruined.

Bonehead was still looking straight ahead. Jupiter reached up and snapped the trigger of the hidden camera. Bonehead did turn and glance at him then. But it didn't matter now. The First Investigator's new invention had achieved its secret purpose. Bonehead couldn't know his picture had been taken.

"Okay, you can drop back now," Jupe told Gordon Harker.

As the limousine slowed and fell behind the sports car, Jupe was already unfastening the camera from the lapel of his jacket. He handed it to Bob.

"As soon as you've left me off at the television studio, take this back to Headquarters and develop and enlarge it," he said. "I'm afraid you and Mr. Harker will miss the quiz show, but I've got to have a good, big print of that photograph by the time the taping finishes. Bring it up to me onstage, will you, Bob, as soon as the show is over?"

"Sure." Bob took the camera and slipped it into

his pocket. "But how about letting us in on the mystery, Jupe? What did you want to take a picture of Bonehead for?"

As First Investigator, Jupe was often a step ahead of his two friends. He even rather enjoyed puzzling them at times. But he felt that now the moment had come to explain his actions a little.

"It isn't just a picture of Bonehead," he said. "It's a closeup profile of him in an open car on a windy day. Surely you can see the importance of that, can't you?"

"No," Pete admitted. "Frankly, I can't."

"Neither can I," Bob put in.

"His long blond hair," Jupe pointed out. "As you may have noticed, he keeps it carefully combed straight down all the time. But thanks to the wind, I was able to get a photograph of one of his features which he usually keeps hidden. Do you understand now?"

"No," Bob and Pete said in unison.

"What feature are you talking about?" Pete asked.

"His ears," the First Investigator told him. "Bonehead's famous wiggling ears."

12

THE SECOND QUIZ

It was one minute to two. Jupe saw Milton Glass glance anxiously at the clock again. It was the third time he had done it since Jupe had been watching him.

In one minute the second and final "Wee Rogues Quiz Show" was due to start taping and so far only three of the contestants were in their places on the stage. Bonehead, Bloodhound, and Jupe himself. There was no sign of either Footsie or Peggy.

Jupe looked out at the studio audience. Pete was sitting in the back row. He looked as anxious as Glass did. When he saw Jupe looking at him, he shrugged in a puzzled way. Jupe shrugged back. He could think of no explanation for Footsie's absence, but he was deeply worried about Peggy.

His eyes moved to the rear of the audience. Luther Lomax was in his usual place in the control booth. He was wearing his usual shabby gray suit; his white hair was ruffled and there were deep shadows under his eyes. He looked like a tired old man.

The First Investigator's attention was caught by a movement in the aisle. Footsie was hurrying toward the stage. He paused to hand an envelope to Milton Glass, then walked over to take his place among the contestants.

It was exactly two o'clock now, and Peggy was still missing.

Jupe stood up to let Footsie slide into the seat next to him.

"Close thing," Jupe whispered.

"Yeah." Footsie smiled. "I had a message to pick up at Glass's office at the studio and my old motorbike broke down." He fastened his mike to his tie. "What do I care? I haven't a hope of winning the quiz anyway. And I've been making some nice money on the side running errands for the network and the studio."

Jupe's eyes went back to Milton Glass. He was opening the envelope Footsie had handed him. For a moment his brilliant smile dimmed as he read the message inside. Then his white teeth flashed again. He gave the ready signal to the control room and turned to face the audience.

"I'm afraid I have some rather disappointing news for you all," he said. "I've just received a note from one of our contestants, Peggy. I think I'd better read it to you." He paused for a second, looking down at the sheet of paper he was holding in his hand.

" 'Dear Mr. Glass,' " he read aloud. " 'I'm sorry to let you all down like this. But since my picture's been in the papers I've been having a rough time here with people recognizing me and bothering me on the street just as they did all those years ago. I don't have a chance of winning that quiz-show prize money anyway, so I've decided to drop out and go home to San Francisco. At least people leave me alone there. My very best regards to you and to all the Wee Rogues. . . .' "

Glass paused again.

"It's signed 'Pretty Peggy.' "

There was a murmur from the audience. It was a murmur of sympathy, Jupiter felt.

"Well, if you're watching us, Peggy," Milton Glass went on, "I can only say we're all sorry about the decision you've made. It was a great pleasure having you with us. And we'll all miss you very much."

There was a hearty round of applause.

Glass held up both hands to hush the audience. "And now, on with the show. The second and final 'Wee Rogues Quiz Show,'" he announced.

The lights went down. Jupe forced himself to look at the screen as the two minutes of edited film began.

His mind was too busy to concentrate on it, but even though he gave it only half his attention, his trained investigator's memory recorded all the important points in the brief scenes that flashed in front of his eyes.

Flapjack stole a dog for Mr. Trouble. Peggy drank a strawberry milk shake through a striped straw. Bonehead and Bloodhound started a campfire in the woods to roast corn. Footsie dived into a lake that was only three inches deep. Baby Fatso was trapped in the burning woods. Bloodhound bandaged Footsie's head with a checkered tablecloth. Peggy rescued Baby Fatso from the fire. . . .

The other half of the First Investigator's mind was busy thinking about Peggy. He didn't believe she had written that note. She would never have signed it Pretty Peggy. She hated that name as much as he hated the name Baby Fatso.

Besides, she hadn't gone home. She hadn't checked out of her hotel. And she had been missing all morning.

It looked to Jupe, in fact, as though Peggy was in real danger. Someone was holding her somewhere against her will. The same someone who had forged that note in her name. The same someone who had called Jupe at Headquarters that morning.

" 'She's quite safe at the moment. I just wanted to warn you, she won't be safe much longer. . . . Not if you win that quiz today, Baby Fatso.' "

The two minutes of film ended. The lights went on again.

Jupe glanced at the electronic scoreboard. He had forty-five points. Bonehead had forty. Peggy thirty-five. Bloodhound and Footsie were far behind. He made a quick calculation. He would have to volunteer at least three times.

Milton Glass had swiveled in his chair to face the contestants.

With Peggy gone, Bonehead was asked the first question.

"What was unusual about the straw Pretty Peggy was drinking through?"

"It was striped," Bonehead shot back. "Red,

white, and blue." Applause. Five points for Bonehead. He was tied with Jupe now.

Bloodhound's turn.

"What kind of a milk shake was she drinking?"

Bloodhound hesitated. Jupe's hand shot up an
instant before Bonehead's.

"Chocolate?" Bloodhound suggested in his casual good-humored way.

"Oh no," shouted one of the onlookers.

"I'm terribly sorry," said Glass. "And now we
have a volunteer." Milton Glass beamed at Jupe.

The First Investigator pretended to hesitate. He
knew the answer, of course. It was a strawberry
milk shake.

"Gee, I thought it was chocolate too," Jupe said.
The crowd groaned. He had lost five points. He
went on losing them. When it was his own turn to
answer a question and he was asked what Bloodhound had used as a bandage for Footsie's head, he
pretended to hesitate again.

"A tissue?" he suggested. There were whispers in
the audience.

By the beginning of the fifth and final round,
Bonehead was way ahead with sixty-five points. He
came up with the right answer on his next turn.
Bloodhound and Footsie missed. It was Jupe's last
turn.

"Well, here's an easy one for you," Glass told him in his friendly way. "What did Flapjack steal for Mr. Trouble?"

Jupe glanced at the scoreboard again before answering. By volunteering the wrong answer three times he had managed to lose fifteen points without gaining a single one. He was five points behind Peggy now.

"A pussycat," he said. There were loud groans from the crowd.

"No, I'm afraid not. It was a dog."

The questioning was over.

Milton Glass went into his big production of reading the final scores for the cameras. There was applause from the audience.

Bonehead had won with seventy points. By volunteering and giving the wrong answer three times, Jupiter Jones had managed to reduce his own score to thirty. So even though she had missed this second quiz show altogether, Peggy was now second with thirty-five points.

All three cameras moved in on the smiling Bonehead as he was handed a check for twenty thousand dollars. The First Investigator didn't even bother to watch. He was staring out over the audience, waiting for Bob.

At last Jupe saw him hurrying down the aisle,

followed by Pete. Bob nipped up the stairs onto the stage. He was holding a large manila envelope, which he handed to Jupe.

"It turned out fine," he whispered. "Clear as a full moon."

As Bob returned to his seat, Jupe opened the envelope and slid out the large glossy print inside. It had turned out even better than he had dared to hope. A superb photograph of Bonehead, his hair streaming back in the wind.

His exposed left ear was in perfect focus.

"Ladies and gentlemen," chirped Milton Glass. "I now have the great privilege of presenting"— there was a drumroll from off stage—"the valuable presents all the contestants have won."

The audience whispered in excited anticipation. Jupe put the photograph back in its envelope and prepared to be on camera again.

"To show our appreciation to the Wee Rogues for making these quiz shows possible," Glass ran on. "Trixie, if you please."

The same scantily clad young woman who had appeared on the talk show walked onstage. She was carrying another gold-wrapped box. Jupe raised an eyebrow. This time she and the box were accompanied by a uniformed security guard.

Glass unwrapped the box again, chattering non-stop. At last he said, ". . . a valuable sterling-silver loving cup for each contestant." The crowd oohed and aahed while each of the four Rogues went up to receive his cup.

"Peggy's cup," continued Glass, "will be mailed to her home. Thanks again, Peg, if you're watching. And now it's time to say to the Rogues, to our studio audience, and to you folks at home . . . so long for now."

Milton Glass waved to the camera, his teeth shining as if they would short themselves out. A round of applause, and the show was over.

The cameras stopped rolling. The contestants moved off. Bonehead was standing on the other side of the stage. Milton Glass, Bloodhound, Footsie, the camera crews, and several members of the audience were grouped around him, congratulating him on his victory.

With the other two Investigators close behind him, Jupiter pushed his way through the group until he was facing the young blond man in the leather jacket. He held out the photograph.

"Is this you?" he asked.

"Why?" Bonehead glanced at the picture in an uneasy, puzzled way. But it was impossible for him to pretend that it wasn't his face in the photograph. Everyone standing there could see at once that it was. "Yeah, sure. That's me," he admitted. "Why?"

"Because, for once, your hair wasn't hiding your ears, that's why," Jupe told him. He turned to Milton Glass, who was standing beside him. "People's faces change a lot as they grow older," he explained. "Bloodhound's and Footsie's and mine have changed so much you wouldn't recognize us as the kids who acted in those *Wee Rogues* comedies. Right?"

"Right," Bloodhound agreed. Milton Glass nodded.

"But there's one thing that never changes," Jupe went on. "That's the form and shape of a person's ears. Bonehead had very unusual ears with big dangling lobes. But the person in the picture here—the person who just won that prize money— has completely different ears. He has small lobes that are attached to his face."

The young man in the leather jacket took a threatening step forward. He tried to grab the picture out of Jupe's hand. Bloodhound put up his arm and held him back.

"What are you trying to say?" Bonehead sputtered.

"I'm saying," the First Investigator told him

calmly, "that you were never one of the Wee Rogues. You had no right to compete in these quiz shows. And I think Mr. Glass will agree with me that you are automatically disqualified from winning the prize money. Because—"

Jupe waved the photograph he was holding.

"Because this picture proves beyond any doubt that whoever you are, you cannot possibly be Bonehead!"

13

KIDNAPPED!

They were all gathered in a big office in the network building: the impostor who had pretended to be Bonehead, Milton Glass, Luther Lomax, the Three Investigators, Bloodhound, Footsie, and a security guard from the television company.

Milton Glass was sitting behind the desk. In front of him was the photograph Jupe had taken. The fake Bonehead was lounging in a chair facing Glass. The others were grouped around him in other chairs.

"Okay," the young man in the leather jacket said, "so I blew it. I let Baby Fatso here take a picture of me with my hair off my ears." He glanced at Jupe. "I told you I knew you weren't dumb. But I guess you're even smarter than I thought you were.

"Big deal." The impostor shrugged his broad shoulders. "It was worth a try. Twenty thousand bucks. That's a lot of bread. And I almost got away with it. I'm not gonna even try to run to a bank with the check—you'd just stop payment."

He reached in his pocket and took out the check for the prize money he had won on the quiz show. He looked at it for a moment with a glint of regret in his sharp eyes. Then he crunched it up and tossed it across the desk to Milton Glass.

"Let's have the cup, too," said Luther Lomax, confidence seeping back into his voice again.

The fake Bonehead regretfully took it out of his leather jacket and smacked it down on the desk.

"Who are you?" the security man asked in a flat voice. "What's your real name?"

"What's it to you?" The impostor shrugged again. "Who cares what my name is? I'm just like thousands of others in this town. I'm an out-of-work actor. A pretty good actor too."

The First Investigator privately agreed with him about that. He was certainly a better actor than the real Bonehead had ever been.

Milton Glass straightened out the crumpled check and tucked it away in his pocket. "Who put you up to it?" he asked.

"Nobody." The impostor's voice was as hard and

confident as ever. "Nobody put me up to it. I'd been watching *The Wee Rogues* on television, reading about them in the papers. I'd been at school for a while with the kid who played Bonehead in the series, and I knew he'd disappeared years ago. I figured he was probably dead. Got run over or something. He was dumb enough to get run over by a lawn mower.

"I looked enough like him except for my ears," he went on. "And it gave me an idea. At first I was just trying to cash in on the publicity. I thought I might get a job out of it. An acting job. Then the network came up with that quiz-show stunt, and I decided to go for it. Who wouldn't? Twenty thousand smackers."

There was silence. Milton Glass was still smiling, but in a doubtful way.

"So what are you going to do about it?" the fake Bonehead challenged him.

"We're going to hand you over to the police," the security man told him. "We're going to bring charges against you for fraud and—"

He broke off. Milton Glass was holding up his hand.

"Not so fast," he said. "Neither the network nor the movie studio wants that kind of publicity. Can you imagine what the newspapers would make out of this?" He flashed his teeth at the security man. "And after all, what harm has been done? We'll be sending a check for twenty thousand to Peggy in San Francisco. And I'm sure she won't ask any questions about it. And as for this young man . . ."

He turned his smile on the impostor.

"Well," he went on, "why don't we just treat the whole thing like a little prank?" He glanced at Luther Lomax. "Okay with you, Luther?"

The elderly director lowered his tired eyes. He ran his fingers through his thin, white hair.

"Sure," he said. "It's okay with me."

Jupiter stood up. At a sign from him the other two Investigators rose to their feet too.

"You can count on us not to talk to the newspapers," Jupe said. It looked as though the meeting would be coming to an end any moment now, and he wanted to get out of there first. He wanted to get down to the parking lot, where Gordon Harker was waiting for him with the limousine. "So if you don't mind, Mr. Glass, we'll be going now."

"Of course." The publicity man stood up too. "And I must say we're all very grateful to you, Jupe." His smile was as cordial as ever, but he didn't sound in the least grateful. "You did a brilliant job of detection. Without your help a serious injustice would have been done. Peggy would have been cheated out of the prize money she so richly deserves."

Jupe thanked him and led Bob and Pete to the door. As he turned to close it behind him, he glanced back into the office. Milton Glass was leaning forward in his chair, smiling in a relieved way at the fake Bonehead, who was smiling now too. Luther Lomax, his eyes still lowered, was picking at a grease spot on his shabby gray suit. The security man was frowning at the window.

The elevator was filled with people. The Three Investigators were silent as they rode down to the street level. It wasn't until they were out in the lobby that Bob and Pete had a chance to express their feelings.

"You're going to let them get away with that?" Pete asked angrily. He couldn't believe it. In all the time they had been friends, he had never known Jupe to walk out on a case and let the crooks go free. And that was what it appeared to Pete that the First Investigator was doing now. It seemed obvious to him that Milton Glass had been a party to the deception from the beginning. Glass had known all along that Bonehead was a fake. That was why he was letting that impostor get away with it.

"Yes," Bob chimed in. He was as shocked and angry as Pete. "And what about Peggy? You told us you were sure she hadn't really gone home to San Francisco. You said you thought she was in danger."

"Yeah," Pete agreed. He was more puzzled than angry now. "What are you thinking of, Jupe?"

The First Investigator pinched his lip. "I'm thinking of Peggy," he said. "I've been thinking about her ever since I got that threatening phone call this morning." He had already told the other two Investigators about that.

"That's why I missed all those questions, lost all those points," he continued, "so that Peggy would win. And I'm still thinking about her." He looked at Bob. "Because you're right. She is in danger. And we've got to save her. Come on."

Without another word he hurried out onto the sidewalk. Bob and Pete followed him.

Gordon Harker was sitting in the limousine in the parking lot, reading a magazine. He put it down as Jupe approached the rear door.

"Where to?" he asked cheerfully.

"Nowhere. Nowhere yet, thanks." Jupe and his two friends got into the back of the car. The First Investigator looked across to where Milton Glass's fancy yellow Citroën was standing. "Do you think you could back up a bit, so we can keep our eyes on that car over there without being seen?" he asked.

"And still be in a position to go after it when it pulls out?"

"Sure."

The chauffeur turned on the ignition and maneuvered the big limousine to the back of the lot where it wouldn't be noticed. From there Harker could still see the whale-shaped nose of the foreign car.

"Are we going to tail Milton Glass now?" he asked in his helpful way.

Jupe nodded absently. He was deep in thought, leaning back in his seat. Bob could see that he intended to remain like that. Silent and mystifying.

"No, you don't," the records man of the team said. "I know you enjoy clamming up like this. But you're not going to get away with it this time. You'd better explain to us what happened up in that office."

"Yeah," Pete agreed. "What's going on?"

"Okay." Jupe sighed, but he was secretly rather pleased that his two friends were insisting on hearing his opinion of the case. It would help him to get it all organized in his own mind. He held up his finger.

"Number one," he said, raising his voice so that Gordon Harker could hear him too. He felt a deep debt of gratitude to the former Flapjack and wanted him to feel he was a trusted member of their investigative team. "When was the last time we saw Peggy?"

"On Hollywood Boulevard last night," Bob reminded him. "When Milton Glass picked her up in his car."

"With Bonehead," Jupe added. "Then this morning Bonehead called me. He was imitating Milton Glass's voice, and he warned me I'd better not win that quiz or Peggy would have an accident. What do you infer from that?"

"That he was holding her somewhere," Bob suggested. "I mean, holding her prisoner. But it couldn't be in his apartment at the Magnolia Arms, could it? There are too many other people living there too. She'd manage to attract their attention somehow."

"Right," Jupe told him.

"But now that she's won the quiz," Pete objected, "and Bonehead's been exposed as a fraud, why should she be in danger any longer? Don't you think he'll just let her go?"

"No, I don't," the First Investigator explained. "Because no matter what he said in that office, Bonehead hasn't been working alone. Someone did put him up to pretending to be one of the Wee Rogues. Because someone had to coach him every step of the way. Tell him every detail of our lives as child actors. Tell him, for instance, that we used to get paid on Fridays in cash. In a brown envelope fastened with a red string. Bonehead could never have found out facts like that by himself. He could never have found out that Mr. Trouble's convertible was a Pierce-Arrow '29. Someone had to tell him all those things."

"So he had an accomplice," Bob put in.

"Yes," the First Investigator told him. "And that accomplice helped him kidnap Peggy. And now they can't let her go. Because she knows who that accomplice is. And because kidnapping is a much more serious charge than fraud. You can go to jail for life for kidnapping someone."

"Milton Glass," Bob said. "Ever since he refused to press charges against Bonehead, I've been sure that Milton Glass was in on the whole thing from the beginning."

"Right, Jupe?" Pete asked. "Peggy's locked up somewhere in Milton Glass's house?"

The First Investigator didn't answer. He was leaning forward in his seat, watching the man who was walking toward the big yellow car. Jupe watched him get into the car and start to ease out of the parking lot.

"No," he said. "Milton Glass is just a publicity

hack, trying to protect the studio and the network. He didn't realize Bonehead was an impostor. *That's* the guy who coached the fake Bonehead, who was able to feed him the right answers before each quiz because he knew every foot of the film. *That's* the guy who helped him kidnap Peggy."

"Who?" Bob and Pete leaned forward too, trying to catch a glimpse of the driver of the yellow car as it paused on the corner of Hollywood Boulevard. Gordon Harker drove the limousine smoothly forward behind it.

"Luther Lomax," the First Investigator said.

14

THE RUINED
MANSION

The yellow car turned off Hollywood Boulevard
and headed into the canyons above Beverly Hills.

Luther Lomax was a slow and cautious driver. It
was easy for Gordon Harker to keep him in sight
while making sure the elderly director would not
notice he was being tailed.

The road wound farther and farther up into the
hills. The houses were far apart now, huge estates
behind stone walls. They were homes that had been
built by movie people in the great days of the motion picture industry. Not so long ago special buses
had driven along these roads on "guided tours of
the stars' homes." Buses filled with admiring tour-
ists, peering in through the gates while the driver
called out the famous names of the people who

lived in the secluded houses behind the high walls.

Jupe knew that most of these houses were now owned by bankers and oil men and Arab sheiks. The movie people had moved down into what was known as "the flatlands" of Beverly Hills.

Gordon Harker slowed. The yellow car had turned in through a pair of open gates. The limousine pulled next to the curb and stopped.

"Well? What do you want to do now?" the chauffeur asked. "Should we go in after him?"

"No. Better not, thanks." The First Investigator opened the rear door and stepped out onto the street. "He's probably got guards and housemen and gardeners. If he sees us coming, he'll be ready for us. If you don't mind waiting here, Mr. Harker, we'll try to scout around a bit. We might be able to get some idea where he's keeping Peggy prisoner."

"Okay." Gordon Harker picked up his magazine. "Good luck. And if you need any help, yell."

Jupiter thanked him. Keeping close to the wall, the Three Investigators crept forward to the gates.

They were still open. No guard had closed them behind Lomax. There was no guard. There was no one else in sight either. Milton Glass's yellow car was parked in front of the great arched doorway of the house.

It looked curiously out of place there. It was the

only thing Jupe could see that did not remind him of a movie about an abandoned southern mansion. One of those old movies like *Gone With the Wind.*

It was still a mansion. The whole front of the house was one great columned porch. A veranda ran along below the upstairs windows. Two wings stretched back from the ends of the building.

But the plaster of the tall columns was chipped and crumbling. Many of the windows were patched or boarded up. The steps that led up to the porch were little more than rubble—broken stones with weeds and bushes pushing their way up between them.

To the right of the gates was a line of trees stretching toward the house. Jupe motioned to his two friends and ran to the nearest tree. The grass was so high beneath the trees that the Three Investigators could crouch down in it, safely hidden, as they moved slowly forward.

"Gosh," Pete said. "You mean someone still lives here?"

Jupe nodded somberly. He was trying to imagine the whole place as it must have been, with well-trimmed lawns and brightly colored beach chairs, with freshly painted white columns and sparkling windows.

How long ago, he wondered. Maybe not more than eight or nine years. With the flash floods and mud slides of southern California, the hot dry sun, and the tropical vegetation, neglected buildings and gardens fell into ruin and decay very fast. At the time Luther Lomax was directing the *Wee Rogues* comedies, this had probably still been an elegant estate like the others in this area of the canyons.

One thing was certain, Jupe decided. It had been a long time since there had been guards or house-men or staff of any kind around here. Lomax was almost surely alone in that house with Peggy.

"Come on," the First Investigator said. "There's no need to scout around anymore. Let's just walk up to the front door and have it out with Lomax."

The other two Investigators agreed. There didn't seem to be much to fear from the elderly director.

There was no bell. Jupe lifted the tarnished brass knocker and banged it down against the tarnished brass plate below it. The door opened at once. Luther Lomax stood there peering out at them.

"Jupiter Jones," he said. "And your two young friends. I've been expecting you. I guess you've come about that reward I promised you for solving the mystery of those silver cups. Come in."

The Three Investigators stepped inside and the

elderly director closed the door after them. They were in a vast, dim hallway. It looked even bigger to Jupe because there was almost no furniture in it—just a couple of canvas chairs and a battered desk.

Jupiter's glance moved to the walls. They were covered with framed photographs of handsome young men and beautiful women. Jupe recognized some of them from old movies on television. They were the great stars of ten, twenty, thirty years ago.

Lomax saw him looking at them. He straightened. For a moment he looked strong and successful, like the faces in the photographs.

"My old friends," he said. "Before the studio insulted my genius by putting me on those ridiculous *Wee Rogues* comedies, I directed some of those stars' greatest pictures. I wouldn't be boasting if I told you that many of them owed their stardom to me." His voice rose, echoing around the walls. He clasped his hands together. "I taught them everything. I molded and fashioned them. I *created* them."

Bob shivered. In spite of the patched broken windows, it wasn't cold in the huge, empty hallway. It was just so creepy, he thought. It was like a tomb, haunted by the ghosts of the past.

"About that reward," Lomax went on in his normal voice. "I don't happen to have much cash on me at the moment, but I'm sure the publicity department—"

"We didn't come about the reward," Jupe interrupted him, and Bob could see that his friend felt as shivery and creepy as he did. "We came to take Peggy home."

"Peggy? You mean Pretty Peggy?" The director unclasped his hands and slipped them into the pockets of his worn jacket. "But what on earth makes you think she's here?"

"We saw you pick her up on Hollywood Boulevard last night," Pete told him. "Peggy and Bonehead got into your car and—"

"But that's ridiculous." Lomax was trying to smile. "I don't even have a car at the moment. My Rolls is being repaired and my—"

"That car outside," Jupe explained. "I guess it belongs to Milton Glass or maybe to the movie studio. But they must have been letting you use it while you were directing the quiz shows. You drove it up here just now. And you were driving it last night when you picked up Peggy and Bonehead."

Lomax was no longer even trying to smile. He made his way to one of the canvas chairs and sat down.

"They wouldn't even give me a limousine," he

said in a tired, plaintive voice. "They were paying me the absolute minimum for directing those quiz shows, and they wouldn't even send a limousine for me. I had to beg Milton to lend me one of his cars. I had to practically threaten him that it wouldn't look very good for the studio or the network if one of their greatest and most famous directors had to try to hitch a ride—"

His voice broke off. He was staring down at his knees. He picked absently at his threadbare trousers. "But I didn't kidnap Peggy," he said. "You're all wrong about that."

"Please, Mr. Lomax," Jupe pleaded softly. "We don't want to make a lot of trouble for you. But we know that Peggy didn't write that note to Milton Glass. We know she didn't drop out of the quiz show of her own free will. And if you won't let us see her and take her home, we're going to have to call the police so they can search the whole—"

"Of course she's here." The director raised his head. That authority was back in his face again. "Peggy is staying in my home as my guest. I'm going to make a great star out of her. I'm going to make her rich and famous." He stood up and indicated the framed photographs on the walls. "Like all those others, who owe everything to me. I'm going to direct Peggy in a great motion picture—"

"Cut it out, you old has-been."

The curt, hard voice had come from the doorway. The Three Investigators turned instantly to face the speaker. The blond young man in the leather jacket took a threatening step forward into the great hall-way.

15

BABY FATSO TURNS THE TABLES

"Cut it out," Bonehead repeated, keeping his eyes on Luther Lomax. "I'm through listening to you. You got me into this mess, using me to steal those cups for you and promising me half their value and that you'd coach me with the right answers and give me half the quiz money. And what did I get out of it? Nothing."

Bonehead looked at Jupe. "It was his idea right from the beginning," he went on. "He saw me in a play I did at a little theater in Hollywood. He came to see me backstage afterward, and he told me what a great actor I was."

Lomax was still standing with his hands in his jacket pockets. He shook his head slightly.

"I was just flattering you," he said. "You have a small talent, but that's all. You could never be a star. Not even with my help."

Bonehead ignored him. He was still looking at Jupe.

"I wasn't going to spill all this in Milton Glass's office," he said. "I knew Lomax had Peggy locked in a room here. And that's a kidnapping charge. I knew the cops would say I was as guilty as he was, even though it was all his idea. I made him promise there wouldn't be any violence. But I did help him set it up. I called Peggy and got her to come to my apartment last night. I told her Milton Glass wanted to talk to us both. But I said that Glass didn't want anyone else to know about it. So I said Glass would pick us up on Hollywood Boulevard."

The First Investigator nodded. What Bonehead had said checked with the facts as he knew them, but he was wondering what the young blond actor was hoping to get in return for this confession.

"We had to get Peggy out of the way so she wouldn't win," Bonehead went on, "and so we'd have a way to make you stop trying."

"What do you want?" Jupe asked.

"A deal," Bonehead told him. "I'll make a deal with you. I'll take you to Peggy. We'll ..." He smiled briefly. "We'll rescue her together. And in return, you back me up. You tell her it was my idea to come here, to set her free. No harm done. She'll listen to you if you tell her the whole story and about the way you made sure she won that quiz money. *You* persuade her not to bring any charges against me."

Jupe looked at Bob and then at Pete. The First Investigator knew he had no authority to make any deals. If Peggy wanted to press charges against Lomax and Bonehead, the law would step in. Once that happened he would have to tell every word of the truth, everything he knew, everything Bonehead had said.

On the other hand, the first, the most important thing, was to get Peggy out of there. After that it would be up to her whether she wanted to go to the police or not. Jupe was still looking at his two friends in a questioning way.

Pete nodded.

Bob hesitated a second longer and then nodded too.

"Okay," Jupe said. "I'll do my best to persuade her that you didn't mean her any real harm. I'll tell her you came here to set her free. But that's all I can promise. After that, it's up to Peggy. Where is she?"

"Upstairs. This way. I saw him lock her in one

of the bedrooms." Bonehead took a quick step forward and then stopped.

Luther Lomax had taken his right hand out of his jacket pocket. He was holding a small black automatic.

"No," the director said. "You're not going to have her. Peggy's going to stay here with me."

He was standing with his feet slightly apart, his head thrown back. He looked exactly the way Jupe remembered him—tall, imposing, a figure of authority.

"I made a child star out of her," he went on in a deep, ringing voice. "And I can do it again. She has the talent. I know she has. And I can bring it out. I can make her a great actress. Together we'll produce a great motion picture. An Oscar winner. We'll both make a superb comeback. We'll both be famous and rich again."

Pete looked at Lomax, measuring the distance between them. One of the Second Investigator's specialties was flying tackles. A headlong leap and a quick grab at an antagonist's knees had gotten the three friends out of some dangerous situations in the past.

But there was no way he could bring it off this time. The director was too far away from him. Before Pete could hope to bring Lomax down, he would have too much time to use that gun he was holding.

Jupe sensed what Pete was thinking. He raised his hand in a gesture of caution.

"Come on, Mr. Lomax," he said in his most persuasive voice. "You don't want to shoot anybody. You're not a killer. You're a great director. You—"

"Don't count on it," Bonehead interrupted curtly. "He's crazy enough to do anything. I know him better than you do. You know what he was going to do with his share of that quiz money? Throw a big party! Invite all those other has-beens he's got up on the walls. The ones who are still alive anyway. Hire a gypsy orchestra. Call in the press and—"

"Quiet!" The director raised his left hand in a commanding way. "Quiet on the set!" he shouted. "Now, all four of you. Get in line. Put your hands on top of your heads."

Bonehead was the first to obey. The others fell in line beside him.

"Now!" Lomax was still shouting. "Right turn, and when I say 'March,' you march straight ahead to that archway there. And down those stairs. Ready?"

Again Bonehead was the first to respond. The Three Investigators nodded too.

"Lights," the director called in his ringing tone, "camera, action. March."

The archway was at the back of the hall. Jupe could see the stone steps leading down from it. They seemed to go a long way down before they turned out of sight. There was probably an old cellar down there, he thought. If Lomax locked them into it, he might be just crazy enough to lose the key, or forget to feed them. And there were no neighbors or employees to hear their screams. Their best chance might be to make a break for it now. He could feel Pete just behind him.

The First Investigator slowed his pace.

"Get on with it," Bonehead called to him in a pleading voice from the back of the line. "Do what he tells you before he shoots me."

Jupe reached the archway and started down the steps.

"March!" Lomax was shouting. "March! March! March—"

His voice broke off. Jupe heard a gasp of fear. Something thudded to the floor with a dead, heavy sound. From long practice the Three Investigators had learned to coordinate their movements like a basketball team. In a second they had scattered out of the line and formed a wide-spaced ring around the back of the hall.

The first thing Jupe saw was the black automatic lying on the floor a few feet from the open front door. Then he saw Lomax. He seemed to be swimming in the air, treading water, his pumping legs and feet well off the ground. A pair of burly arms was holding him up from behind. Two strong black hands were locked together around his waist.

Gordon Harker was very gentle with the elderly director. He was obviously being careful not to hurt him as he carried him across the hallway and sat him down in a canvas chair.

"Now you just sit there quietly, Mr. Lomax," the chauffeur said, holding him down firmly, but still gently, by the shoulders. "Pick up the gun, Jupe. Make sure the safety's on and then put it in your pocket."

Jupe did as he was told. He looked at Bonehead. The young actor was leaning against the wall. His face was very pale and he was trembling slightly.

"Thank you, Mr. Harker," the First Investigator said.

"Think nothing of it," the chauffeur told him. "When I saw that young guy creeping up here and remembered what you had told me about him, I thought I'd better find out what was going on."

"I'm very glad you did." Jupe looked at Bonehead. "Come on. Where's Peggy?"

Still obviously shaken, the young actor led the Three Investigators up the stairs and down to the end of a long dusty corridor. The key was in the outside of the door. Jupe turned it in the lock and stepped into the room.

Peggy was sitting in a chair beside the boarded-up window. There was a wadded handkerchief in her mouth, held there by another handkerchief tied around her head. Her hands were bound behind the back of the chair and her ankles were tied to the chair legs.

Bonehead gave a gasp when he saw her. "I didn't know," he said quietly. "I didn't know he was going to tie her up. If I'd known . . . I would never have helped him get her here."

Jupe believed him. From what he had seen of Bonehead's behavior in the last few minutes, he had realized Bonehead's toughness was nothing but a pose. Underneath it, the young actor had a terror of violence.

The Three Investigators hurried across to Peggy, leaving Bonehead still leaning weakly against the door. Pete and Bob ungagged her while Jupe took out his Swiss army knife and cut the binding ropes.

Peggy shook her head as though to clear it. She

rubbed her wrists and pushed her hair away from her forehead. She carefully stretched her legs and with some difficulty stood up. She smiled.

"Well," she said. "This is funny. Just like one of our old *Wee Rogues* comedies. Except then I was always rescuing you, Jupe. And now you've rescued me."

16

A FAVOR FOR DON

"Peggy was so happy about winning that prize money," Jupe said, "that she decided not to press charges against either Luther Lomax or Bonehead."

"She can afford to go to college now, which is what she's always wanted to do," Bob put in.

"She's planning to start at Berkeley in September," Pete added.

The Three Investigators were sitting around the patio table in Hector Sebastian's enormous living room with its row of windows overlooking the Pacific Ocean. Referring to the notes Bob had made, they had been giving the mystery writer the rundown on their latest case.

Hector Sebastian was comfortably stretched in a long beach chair beside the table. Before he took up writing some years ago, he had suffered a severe leg injury while working as a private detective in New York, and his leg still gave him a little trouble at times.

"So Bonehead's gone back to acting under his own name now?" he inquired.

"He's trying to, anyway," Jupe told him. "Although I don't think he's having much luck. He still has to work as a mechanic for a living."

The First Investigator paused thoughtfully. "It's funny," he said. "It was my memory of the real Bonehead that got me involved in that quiz show in the first place. I disliked him so much as a kid that I wanted to beat him at all costs. But I almost grew to like the young man who impersonated him. I'm sure he never meant Peggy any harm anyway. He was just so desperate for money and discouraged at being an out-of-work actor that he went along with everything Luther Lomax suggested."

"It can be rough making it in this town," Mr. Sebastian agreed. "Speaking of which, what happened to Luther Lomax? Is he still rattling around in his ruined mansion dreaming about the past?"

"No," Pete answered. "He had a complete nervous breakdown when he saw Peggy come downstairs with us after we'd untied her. He kept shouting, 'Quiet on the set,' and 'Lights, camera, action!' Gordon Harker finally managed to calm him down and drive him to a hospital."

The mystery writer shook his head sympathetically. "He was a great director once," he said. "I remember many of his old movies. Is he still in a hospital?"

"No," Jupe explained. "The Motion Picture Association found a comfortable place for him in the mental wing of a home they run for retired movie people. At least he's among some of his old friends there."

"Yes." Mr. Sebastian smiled wryly. "I'm sure he is. There's an old saying in Hollywood: 'You don't have to be crazy to make pictures, but it certainly helps.'

"And Glass was totally innocent of the plot between Bonehead and Lomax?" Mr. Sebastian asked.

"Yes," Jupiter said. "All along, Glass had no knowledge that Bonehead was a phony, that Lomax had stolen the cups, or that the two had kidnapped Peggy. Glass was trying to get promoted at the network by putting on the quiz shows. He didn't want to queer his reputation by exposing Bonehead as a fake once the shows were over."

"What about Footsie and Bloodhound?" Mr. Sebastian went on. "What happened to them?"

"The quiz shows gave Footsie the break he needed," Jupe answered. "He'd been out of work a long time. An athletic-shoe-store chain saw the shows and hired Footsie to do publicity for them—appearances at shopping malls and things like that. He was glad to get the work. And he doesn't need to wear big shoes or act, he just has to talk about their products.

"Bloodhound is going to finish college and then go on to law school. He wants to help young actors and actresses fight for their rights against movie studios and television networks that try to exploit them."

"A worthwhile endeavor," commented Mr. Sebastian.

He glanced toward the kitchen, where the Three Investigators could hear Sebastian's Vietnamese houseman, Hoang Van Don, rattling his pots and pans.

"And Gordon Harker?" Mr. Sebastian asked. "Are you keeping his secret?"

"Of course we are," Pete assured him. "We've never told anyone about him being Flapjack in those old *Wee Rogues* comedies—except you, that is. He'll be totally safe when he goes back to teaching in September."

"Speaking of school"—Mr. Sebastian glanced toward the kitchen again—"Don's been going to school too, lately."

"He has?" Bob asked. "What's he studying?"

"Cordon bleu cooking," Mr. Sebastian explained. "Like a French chef. He's given up all his health food ideas now." He sighed. "It's all complicated sauces and fancy cuisine these days. I must say it's an improvement on seaweed. But it's a little rich for my stomach."

He paused and leaned forward in his beach chair. "I do hope you'll be staying for lunch," he said. "Especially you, Jupe."

Bob and Jupe looked at each other skeptically. They could remember only too well that Don had recently used them as guinea pigs for another exotic French treat—snails. But all three Investigators dutifully said they would be delighted to stay for lunch and try Don's French cooking.

"But why especially me?" Jupe asked.

"Because Don wants a favor from you," Mr. Sebastian said. "And in return he's agreed to cook you anything you want for our lunch. Absolutely *anything*," he added wistfully.

The First Investigator caught the note of wistfulness—it was almost eagerness—in the mystery writer's voice.

"Why don't you decide, Mr. Sebastian?" he suggested helpfully. "Why don't we have something *you* want?"

"I was hoping you'd say that." Mr. Sebastian reached for the cane beside his chair and pushed himself to his feet. "Because I must admit I've got a sort of craving for a nice plain hamburger. Maybe with a thin slice of raw onion on it. But no sauces. Not even ketchup. Just plain ground beef."

The three boys agreed that plain hamburger would be fine.

"But what's the favor Don wants from me?" Jupe asked.

"That's his secret, I'm afraid," Sebastian told him. "But I'm sure it isn't anything to worry about." He turned, leaning on his cane. "I'll just go and tell Don then. Plain hamburger. And in return you promise to do him the favor, Jupe. Whatever it is."

The Three Investigators watched Mr. Sebastian limp across the huge room and around the tall bookcase dividing the living area from the study, on his way to the kitchen.

Sebastian's house in Malibu had once been a restaurant called Charlie's Place, which explained why there was so much open space in it. The writer was gradually converting it into what he called a stately home. He had made some progress since their last visit, Jupe saw. Besides the beach chair he had also added a comfortable-looking couch to the still rather sparse furnishings.

When Sebastian came back, he was smiling eagerly. "Plain hamburger it is," he announced, settling comfortably back into the beach chair. "Don wanted to serve it with a béarnaise sauce, but I told him you like it with no trimmings."

He was silent for a moment, resting his leg. "I've been thinking about your latest case," he said after a moment. "There's only one thing about it that puzzles me."

"Yes?" Jupe asked. "What is it?"

"What made you first suspect Lomax? How did you guess it was the director, rather than Milton Glass or one of the Rogues, who had coached the impostor Bonehead with all the information he would need to pass himself off as the real Bonehead?"

"It was mostly that coincidence with Footsie," the First Investigator explained. "I figured it had to be Bonehead who locked me into the sound stage to keep me away from the first quiz. He was the only one who was surprised to see me show up at the last minute. But what was Footsie doing at the studio that same day at exactly the same time? Why did he go there on his motorbike while I was tailing him in a taxi? That coincidence kept bothering me."

Mr. Sebastian nodded. "It would have bothered me, too," he admitted. "As a detective I was always suspicious of coincidences. But go on, Jupe. When did you finally fit the pieces together?"

"As soon as I got the final clue," Jupe told him. "Just before the second quiz, Footsie told me he had been running errands for the movie studio and the network."

"So you guessed someone had *sent* him to the studio? Right?"

"Right," Jupe agreed. "Someone had sent him there as a decoy. So I *would* follow him. And only one other person besides myself knew at that time that the Three Investigators were looking into the theft—Luther Lomax."

"I see that." Hector Sebastian nodded again. "Lomax got you to come to the network building, pretending he wanted to talk to you about those silver cups. Then as soon as you left him, he sent for Footsie and dispatched him on some errand to the movie studio, knowing you'd see him in the lobby and hoping you'd go after him."

"It was more than a hope," Jupe explained. "Lomax had just told me twice to keep an eye on Footsie. So he could be pretty sure I'd follow him. And of course Lomax already had Bonehead planted at the studio waiting to lock me in the sound stage even if he had to hit me over the head first."

"Yes. It all seems to fit now." Sebastian pushed himself out of his beach chair at the sound of footsteps approaching from the kitchen. "Smells good," he whispered as he sat down at the big patio table.

It did smell good, Jupe thought, remembering all the other meals he had eaten at this table. There had been a time once when Don had served nothing but fast foods, frozen pizza, and fish fingers, the kind that are advertised on late-night TV. After that there had been another phase when everything that came out of the Vietnamese houseman's kitchen had been the kind of foods that are recommended by afternoon TV health gurus—brown rice, raw fish, and seaweed.

He watched Don as he set down a large plate with four king-size hamburgers on it. They looked good too, Jupe decided.

They were good. The best ground beef and slices of raw onion. The First Investigator bit into his with a healthy appetite.

"Okay?" Don asked him.

"Excellent," Jupe complimented him. "First class."

"Okay. Then you do me a favor now?"

"Sure," the First Investigator mumbled with his mouth full of food. "What is it?"

"You very famous. I see you on TV all the time. So you give me your autograph, please."

Don reached into the pocket of his white coat and pulled out a leather-bound autograph book and placed it beside Jupe's plate.

"Sure." Jupe swallowed a piece of onion and took out his pen. It seemed a very small favor for such a good hamburger. "What do you want me to write? The First Investigator? Or just Jupiter Jones?"

"No. No." Don shook his head firmly. "You put famous name. Okay?" Jupe closed his eyes briefly and sighed. Then he leaned over the book.

With very best wishes to Hoang Van Don, he inscribed. He took a deep breath and added his famous name, as he had been asked to.

From Baby Fatso, the First Investigator wrote.

THE THREE INVESTIGATORS MYSTERY SERIES

NOVELS

The Secret of Terror Castle
The Mystery of the Stuttering Parrot
The Mystery of the Whispering Mummy
The Mystery of the Green Ghost
The Mystery of the Vanishing Treasure
The Secret of Skeleton Island
The Mystery of the Fiery Eye
The Mystery of the Silver Spider
The Mystery of the Screaming Clock
The Mystery of the Moaning Cave
The Mystery of the Talking Skull
The Mystery of the Laughing Shadow
The Secret of the Crooked Cat
The Mystery of the Coughing Dragon
The Mystery of the Flaming Footprints
The Mystery of the Nervous Lion
The Mystery of the Singing Serpent
The Mystery of the Shrinking House
The Secret of Phantom Lake
The Mystery of Monster Mountain
The Secret of the Haunted Mirror
The Mystery of the Dead Man's Riddle
The Mystery of the Invisible Dog
The Mystery of Death Trap Mine
The Mystery of the Dancing Devil
The Mystery of the Headless Horse
The Mystery of the Magic Circle
The Mystery of the Deadly Double
The Mystery of the Sinister Scarecrow
The Secret of Shark Reef
The Mystery of the Scar-Faced Beggar
The Mystery of the Blazing Cliffs

(*Continued on next page*)

The Mystery of the Purple Pirate
The Mystery of the Wandering Cave Man
The Mystery of the Kidnapped Whale
The Mystery of the Missing Mermaid
The Mystery of the Two-Toed Pigeon
The Mystery of the Smashing Glass
The Mystery of the Trail of Terror
The Mystery of the Rogues' Reunion
The Mystery of the Creep-Show Crooks

FIND YOUR FATE™ MYSTERIES

The Case of the Weeping Coffin
The Case of the Dancing Dinosaur

PUZZLE BOOKS

The Three Investigators' Book of Mystery Puzzles